Under the Black Ensign

SELECTED FICTION WORKS BY
L. RON HUBBARD

FANTASY
The Case of the Friendly Corpse

Death's Deputy

Fear

The Ghoul

The Indigestible Triton

Slaves of Sleep & The Masters of Sleep

Typewriter in the Sky

The Ultimate Adventure

SCIENCE FICTION
Battlefield Earth

The Conquest of Space

The End Is Not Yet

Final Blackout

The Kilkenny Cats

The Kingslayer

The Mission Earth Dekalogy*

Ole Doc Methuselah

To the Stars

ADVENTURE
The Hell Job series

WESTERN
Buckskin Brigades

Empty Saddles

Guns of Mark Jardine

Hot Lead Payoff

A full list of L. Ron Hubbard's
novellas and short stories is provided at the back.

*Dekalogy—a group of ten volumes

L. RON HUBBARD

Under the Black Ensign

GALAXY
PRESS

Contents

FOREWORD   vii

UNDER THE BLACK ENSIGN   1

STORY PREVIEW:
TWENTY FATHOMS DOWN   85

GLOSSARY   93

L. RON HUBBARD
IN THE GOLDEN AGE
OF PULP FICTION   105

THE STORIES FROM THE
GOLDEN AGE   117

Stories from Pulp Fiction's
Golden Age

A ND it *was* a golden age.
The 1930s and 1940s were a vibrant, seminal time for a gigantic audience of eager readers, probably the largest per capita audience of readers in American history. The magazine racks were chock-full of publications with ragged trims, garish cover art, cheap brown pulp paper, low cover prices—and the most excitement you could hold in your hands.

"Pulp" magazines, named for their rough-cut, pulpwood paper, were a vehicle for more amazing tales than Scheherazade could have told in a million and one nights. Set apart from higher-class "slick" magazines, printed on fancy glossy paper with quality artwork and superior production values, the pulps were for the "rest of us," adventure story after adventure story for people who liked to *read*. Pulp fiction authors were no-holds-barred entertainers—real storytellers. They were more interested in a thrilling plot twist, a horrific villain or a white-knuckle adventure than they were in lavish prose or convoluted metaphors.

The sheer volume of tales released during this wondrous golden age remains unmatched in any other period of literary history—hundreds of thousands of published stories in over nine hundred different magazines. Some titles lasted only an issue or two; many magazines succumbed to paper shortages during World War II, while others endured for decades yet. Pulp fiction remains as a treasure trove of stories you can read, stories you can love, stories you can remember. The stories were driven by plot and character, with grand heroes, terrible villains, beautiful damsels (often in distress), diabolical plots, amazing places, breathless romances. The readers wanted to be taken beyond the mundane, to live adventures far removed from their ordinary lives—and the pulps rarely failed to deliver.

In that regard, pulp fiction stands in the tradition of all memorable literature. For as history has shown, good stories are much more than fancy prose. William Shakespeare, Charles Dickens, Jules Verne, Alexandre Dumas—many of the greatest literary figures wrote their fiction for the readers, not simply literary colleagues and academic admirers. And writers for pulp magazines were no exception. These publications reached an audience that dwarfed the circulations of today's short story magazines. Issues of the pulps were scooped up and read by over thirty million avid readers each month.

Because pulp fiction writers were often paid no more than a cent a word, they had to become prolific or starve. They also had to write aggressively. As Richard Kyle, publisher and editor of *Argosy*, the first and most long-lived of the pulps, so pointedly explained: "The pulp magazine writers, the best of them, worked for markets that did not write for critics or attempt to satisfy timid advertisers. Not having to answer to anyone other than their readers, they wrote about human beings on the edges of the unknown, in those new lands the future would explore. They wrote for what we would become, not for what we had already been."

Some of the more lasting names that graced the pulps include H. P. Lovecraft, Edgar Rice Burroughs, Robert E. Howard, Max Brand, Louis L'Amour, Elmore Leonard, Dashiell Hammett, Raymond Chandler, Erle Stanley Gardner, John D. MacDonald, Ray Bradbury, Isaac Asimov, Robert Heinlein—and, of course, L. Ron Hubbard.

In a word, he was among the most prolific and popular writers of the era. He was also the most enduring—hence this series—and certainly among the most legendary. It all began only months after he first tried his hand at fiction, with L. Ron Hubbard tales appearing in *Thrilling Adventures, Argosy, Five-Novels Monthly, Detective Fiction Weekly, Top-Notch, Texas Ranger, War Birds, Western Stories*, even *Romantic Range*. He could write on any subject, in any genre, from jungle explorers to deep-sea divers, from G-men and gangsters, cowboys and flying aces to mountain climbers, hard-boiled detectives and spies. But he really began to shine when he turned his talent to science fiction and fantasy of which he authored nearly fifty novels or novelettes to forever change the shape of those genres.

Following in the tradition of such famed authors as Herman Melville, Mark Twain, Jack London and Ernest Hemingway, Ron Hubbard actually lived adventures that his own characters would have admired—as an ethnologist among primitive tribes, as prospector and engineer in hostile climes, as a captain of vessels on four oceans. He even wrote a series of articles for *Argosy,* called "Hell Job," in which he lived and told of the most dangerous professions a man could put his hand to.

Finally, and just for good measure, he was also an accomplished photographer, artist, filmmaker, musician and educator. But he was first and foremost a *writer,* and that's the L. Ron Hubbard we come to know through the pages of this volume.

This library of Stories from the Golden Age presents the best of L. Ron Hubbard's fiction from the heyday of storytelling, the Golden Age of the pulp magazines. In these eighty volumes, readers are treated to a full banquet of 153 stories, a kaleidoscope of tales representing every imaginable genre: science fiction, fantasy, western, mystery, thriller, horror, even romance—action of all kinds and in all places.

Because the pulps themselves were printed on such inexpensive paper with high acid content, issues were not meant to endure. As the years go by, the original issues of every pulp from *Argosy* through *Zeppelin Stories* continue crumbling into brittle, brown dust. This library preserves the L. Ron Hubbard tales from that era, presented with a distinctive look that brings back the nostalgic flavor of those times.

L. Ron Hubbard's Stories from the Golden Age has something for every taste, every reader. These tales will return you to a time when fiction was good clean entertainment and the most fun a kid could have on a rainy afternoon or the best thing an adult could enjoy after a long day at work.

Pick up a volume, and remember what reading is supposed to be all about. Remember curling up with a *great story*.

—Kevin J. Anderson

KEVIN J. ANDERSON *is the author of more than ninety critically acclaimed works of speculative fiction, including The Saga of Seven Suns, the continuation of the Dune Chronicles with Brian Herbert, and his* New York Times *bestselling novelization of L. Ron Hubbard's* Ai! Pedrito!

Under the Black Ensign

CHAPTER ONE

Aboard the Terror

T HE marlinespike was inoffensive enough. In capable hands it might possibly have laid a man out. But Tom Bristol had shown few signs of wanting to lay anyone out, and if he had, it is certain that he would not have used a short piece of wood for the purpose. And yet that marlinespike was to be Tom Bristol's passport to piracy.

He was working in the crosstrees of the mizzentop, hanging on with his toes far above a restless deck, using the spike to splice a length of line which had parted in the storm just past.

From his vantage point he could see the swelling reaches of the serene Caribbean, blue and deceptively cool in the morning sunshine. Far to the west he could see a blue smudge—the mountains of St. Kitts. To the south he had seen the soft whiteness of a sail, but as he was not the lookout, he had paid it no further attention.

Besides, in these busy days of 1680, a man would soon grow hoarse crying every ship in sight. And the British man-o'-war was not interested in immediate combat. The HMS *Terror*—five hundred tons, seventy cannon—was concentrating on the task of taking the Lord High Governor of Nevis back to his island, where he would marry the long-expected Lady Jane Campbell.

When Tom Bristol took in the horizons, a close observer might have noticed a certain hunted look flickering in his eyes—the look of a caged leopard angrily pacing behind bars. It was not prominent, that look, but it was there.

Tom Bristol's belt creaked against the spar and his hands were busy at their task. His bare back rippled as he moved his arms. He thrust the marlinespike between hempen strands, and then glanced down at the deck below.

Several men were standing beside the mizzenmast, and the sun played over their gold lace and polished steel in a blinding fanfare of light. In their center was the Lord High Governor. All Bristol could see of this personage was a circle of black hat brim and the extremity of his paunch.

Something about the way the Lord High Governor tried to brace himself expertly against the roll of the ship—an effort which was succeeding ill—excited Bristol's silent laughter.

The marlinespike, none too tightly held, slid out unobserved. Bristol caught sight of it as it flashed down, far out of reach.

Like a bomb it swooped toward the deck, straight for the Lord High Governor. Bristol gripped the spar, suddenly sick with dread. It seemed that the spike fell forever, but still he could find no time to cry out. The clatter as it struck the white planking beside the Lord High Governor might as well have been a cannon shot.

The officers leaped back. With a shrill scream the Lord High Governor threw his hands across his face—a gesture far from necessary, now that the danger had passed.

Wrathful eyes glared up into the rigging. Bristol stared back, forgetting to breathe. He was not a timid man, far from

4

it, but he knew his immediate fate just as well as if it had been already announced.

Lieutenant Ewell's roar was louder than a lion's. "Come out of that, you lubber! Get down here!"

Bristol gripped a stay and slid to the deck. He stood up and faced the officers. The Lord High Governor shook with rage.

"You blackguard! You insolent whelp!" shouted the governor. "Trying to murder me? 'Od's wounds, what have you to say for yourself?"

"My marline—" Bristol began, his voice quite steady.

"Shut up!" cried the governor. "It's attempted murder, that's what it is! Attempted murder! You're in the pay of France to kill me. I see how it is now. I see how it is!"

Captain Mannville, his arrogant face rimmed by a silvery beard, stared holes into Bristol. "We've had trouble with you before, my man. You realize, of course, that your act will not pass without punishment."

Bristol glanced at the others. Their faces were fat and red with soft living, but for all that, the hardness there, those merciless eyes, had sent many a sailor groveling to the deck before them.

Not that this was a particularly cruel set of officers. Perhaps they were even more kindly than the average of the Royal Navy. But this was 1680, and the tide of lust for empire had swung high in the great nations of the world. Human life was nothing. Compassion was almost forgotten. Britain was setting herself to rule the seas, and Spain was setting the example for bestiality.

The Lord High Governor—late of the London courts, where he had been Sir Charles Stukely, gentleman-in-waiting to the King—planted his feet wide against the persistent annoyance of a swinging deck and breathed hard, as though trying to stifle ungentlemanly wrath.

"Flogging takes it out of them," said Sir Charles. "If we let this insult pass, God knows the results upon the rest of this mangy scum."

Captain Mannville nodded. "Ah, yes. Flogging. Bristol, stand to the mast and prepare yourself for a hundred lashes."

Bristol's steadiness deserted him. He stepped back, found the rail, and supported himself with it. His face was a little gray through his dark tan. The brisk trade wind was in his light brown hair, ruffling it.

"A . . . a hundred lashes, sir? My God, it's death!" Through his mind ran the scenes of other floggings. Thus far he had escaped that ever handy cat-o'-nine, used in all navies to maintain discipline. No man had lived through a hundred lashes.

"A hundred lashes!" cried Sir Charles. "Perhaps that will teach the fool to respect the persons of his betters. That murderously thrown belaying pin might have snuffed out my life!"

A marlinespike is hardly a belaying pin. Something in the remark gave Bristol strength. After all, he, Tom Bristol, was a sailor, and this Sir Charles was a landlubber. The contempt possessed by all sailors came to Bristol's aid.

Pushing himself away from the rail and standing up straight, he looked the Lord High Governor in the eye. "It happens, sirrah, that the marlinespike fell quite by accident. But had I known that it would fall, I am certain that I would have pitched it more accurately."

Sir Charles' face became dangerously purple again. He grew in size, his fat width puffed out, his voice broke through the bonds of his rage.

"You . . . you address me as 'sirrah'? You intimate that . . ." He was speechless. His eyes threatened to pop out on his cheeks.

"Silence, Bristol!" said Captain Mannville. "For that insolence you shall receive an additional hundred lashes."

Bristol turned on him. His eyes were reckless now. There was something wild and vibrant about him as he stood there, like a fine steel blade quivering.

"A hundred lashes more?" cried Bristol, almost laughing. "I'll be dead in the first seventy-five! And while I'm still able to talk, Mannville, there's something I have to say which might interest you."

"Silence!" cried Mannville, his hand on the butt of his pistol.

"Go ahead and shoot! The quicker the better!"

Bristol was aware of faces outside the circle. Men of the crew were staring at him, unable to believe that anyone would have the courage to speak thus to *gentlemen*.

"Five months ago," said Bristol, "I went ashore in Liverpool. Before I even entered a tavern, I was set upon by your press gang and dragged out to this ship. When I tried to protest, you had me thrown in irons.

"Mannville, it has never made any difference to the Royal Navy who manned its men-o'-war. In my home port, I am listed as dead. My ship sailed without me.

"Press ganging may have some justification when applied to men on the beach, but it happened, Mannville, that I was first mate of the bark *Randolph* out of Maryland."

"Silence!" cried Mannville again. He was having some difficulty looking this man in the eye, and that fact did little to improve his temper.

"I demand that this insolent wretch be punished instantly!" bellowed the Lord High Governor. "First he tries to murder me, and then he dares to speak this way to officers of the King!"

Mannville stepped back and made a sign to two British marines. They fell upon Bristol and carried him swiftly to the mast. Two lines were ready there for any man who might be unlucky enough to be flogged. These were immediately made fast to Bristol's wrists.

Facing the mast, his arms drawn above him painfully tight, he felt the hot sun on his bare back. He saw the quartermaster step forward. In the quartermaster's hand was the cat-o'-nine.

Originally the cat-o'-nine-tails was merely a collection of thongs held together in a short handle. But the Royal Navy had changed all that. This cat-o'-nine had brass wire wound about the ends of the thongs, and the brass was tipped by pellets of lead.

Wielded by brawny quartermasters, the cat-o'-nine was responsible for more deaths than scurvy or gunshot.

The captain stepped back. Sir Charles moved a little closer.

The Lord High Governor's eyes were brittle hard, like polished agate.

The lash went back with a swift, singing sound. Bristol clenched his teeth and shut his eyes, expecting the white-hot flash of pain.

Bristol clenched his teeth and shut his eyes,
expecting the white-hot flash of pain.

CHAPTER TWO

Scarlet Rapier and Plumed Hat

THE time-honored cry of the sea floated down to them from the foretop. "Sail ho!" All eyes went aloft. The lash was momentarily forgotten. The sail must be very close, otherwise it would not have been announced.

"Where away?" shouted Mannville.

"Off the starboard, coming across our bows!"

Men leaped to the rail. The haze of light cast up by the sun on water momentarily blinded them. And then they saw the ship. It was sailing against the morning sun, full-rigged, tall-masted, gilded sterncastle sparkling. It was a bark of about sixty guns. Against the light, its sails looked black.

Even as they stared at it, a roll of bunting went up the truck and burst. Its identity was unmistakable. A grinning skull against an ebon field.

"A pirate!" cried Lieutenant Ewell.

"The nerve of him!" said Mannville. "Showing his colors to a British man-o'-war! Trumpeter! Sound quarters! We attack immediately!"

Bristol, by turning his head away from the mast, saw the scurrying men about him. He looked down at the cat-o'-nine. It lay curled like a den of snakes beside his feet. He kicked it away from him.

Men swarmed into the shrouds. The crack of unfurled canvas sounded like far-off cannon fire. The man-o'-war shuddered under the impact of wind. One rail swooped down and stayed there. The waves began to whip past as the bows pointed out the new course. Spray leaped, glistening like pearls, over the forecastle head.

The Lord High Governor, insignificant in all this sudden bustle about the black guns, slid aft along the rail, heading for the protection of the after cabins. Bristol watched him with a thin smile.

Powder monkeys scampered out of the hold with their leather powder buckets. Men sweated as they carried extra shot to the racks. Gun captains blew feverishly upon sputtering matches, and tuned an ear for the command to fire.

The pirate bark, only half its canvas set, held its own. It was less than a cable's length away. The foamy wake spread out behind it across the restless waves. It was taking full advantage of the smart breeze.

Bristol, forgotten in the turmoil, watched the pirate. Only ten years before, the British ship would have dipped its own colors and continued smoothly upon its way. But now the cry was "Down with buccaneers!"

Driven out of Port Royal by a suddenly righteous government, the buccaneer had been forced to turn pirate. Before that, he was the only united power against Spain—and he had made the *dons* scurry before him, leaving the English many spoils.

But England and France and Denmark and Holland had forgotten that the buccaneer had ever been of use. They were united against him, even though they themselves were fighting a guerrilla warfare against one another.

Bristol watched the bark. It made little difference to him what happened to the pirate. This was merely a respite. If a shot didn't cut him down, and if the cannon on either side of him didn't break loose or explode and thereby kill him, the quartermaster would return to the flogging.

The bark seemed nearer. It was certainly taking its time about getting away from them. Perhaps—and you never could tell about pirates—perhaps this vessel was laying some kind of trap. But there was never any loot aboard a man-o'-war. What did the pirate want?

Abruptly the bark luffed, spilling the wind from its flapping canvas. It slowed down. The man-o'-war, still under full sail, lunged ahead. Too late Captain Mannville saw that he had been guilty of a tactical error. Before the man-o'-war could be turned aside, it presented an oblique to the pirate broadside.

Twenty cannon spat flame and iron, and the pirate heeled under the recoil of its own guns. Clouds of powder smoke mushroomed up through the spilling sails.

The man-o'-war shuddered. The grape and canister had whipped through the rigging, leaving the sails in tatters. The mainmast began to tremble. Canvas came down in a snowy shroud. Lines and gear slithered to the cluttered decks.

The gun captains touched their matches. The sullen hiss of burning fuses was loud. But the delay between ignition and firing was fatal. Responding to the late order, the man-o'-war slipped sideways to the bark. Her cannon hammered out at an empty ocean.

Blackened by smoke and stunned slightly by a r'yal spar, Bristol saw the gunners slaving to reload. It required half an hour for that tedious operation.

Mannville was striving to jibe around and loose his larboard broadside. The pirate darted in. Mountains of whipping sails loomed through the acrid fog. Bristol saw a bowsprit lunge across the rail. He could see scarlet bandannas and the white lightning of ready cutlasses.

The battle cry of the pirates drowned all else. They sprang down, an avalanche of furious color, to the decks of the man-o'-war. The British snatched up pikes and swords and belaying pins. Faces pale with fear, they strove to stem the flow of fearless men.

A wail went up from the sterncastle. The sound spread, grew in volume. Captain Mannville's raging bellow hacked through the tumult.

"Who struck those colors?"

But it was too late. The British ensign was a heap of dirtied bunting on the deck. The sailors threw down their weapons and crowded back against the port rail, screaming for quarter. Mannville dropped his sword and stood back, understanding that it was useless to go on.

Through the wraiths of powder smoke came a gigantic figure, like the devil himself striding through the fumes of brimstone. On his head was a plumed hat and about his shoulders there swirled a red cloak. A naked rapier, dripping scarlet, was held in his bejeweled hand.

The rapier jerked toward the crowd of sailors. "Herd them together. Who's in command here?"

14

The battle cry of the pirates drowned all else.
They sprang down, an avalanche of furious color,
to the decks of the man-o'-war.

Mannville stepped forward, head down, eyes on the planks. "I surrender and ask for quarter."

"Huh. Good! Avast, lads—scurry through the aft cabins and see what's there. Lively, now!" The buccaneer strode toward the captives, raking them with hard black eyes. "Not a man among the lot of you, is there?"

No one spoke immediately. They swallowed the insult. From the sterncastle came a group of men, glittering cutlasses poking gleefully at the back of the Lord High Governor.

"Belay that!" barked the pirate commander.

Sir Charles, seeing the buccaneer, immediately fell quivering like jelly to his knees. "I pray you, give me quarter! Do not kill me!"

"And who the hell might you be?"

"Sir Charles Stukely, Lord High Governor of Nevis. The King will ransom me. Do not put me to death!"

"So you think the King might ransom you, eh? He'd be a fool to pay more than a ha'penny!" No mercy in those chill eyes. Only a twinkle of amusement.

The Lord High Governor's teeth chattered like a signal ratchet. He lifted his hands beseechingly. The pirate abruptly turned his back.

Bristol, forgetting that he'd have the dubious honor of dying in a few minutes at pirate hands, laughed sharply. For the first time, the buccaneers saw him.

A young midshipman, smooth of face, probably—or so thought Bristol—about fifteen, came close to him. The midshipman's sword quickly severed the ropes that bound him. Bristol rubbed his arms.

*From the sterncastle came a group of men, glittering
cutlasses poking gleefully at the back of the
Lord High Governor.*

"And what the hell was happening to you?" rapped the buccaneer commander.

In a voice singularly gentle, the midshipman replied, "Where are your eyes, Bryce? The man was being flogged at the time of attack."

"Flogged, eh?" said Bryce. "Damn my eyes, but I haven't forgotten a few floggings given me! What's the cause, lad?"

Bristol jerked a thumb at Sir Charles. "I almost stove in his skull with a marlinespike."

"What ho!" cried Bryce. "That's good going, lad! What's your name?"

"Tom Bristol, late first mate of the bark *Randolph,* out of Maryland."

Bryce turned to the midshipman. "And how's that for luck, Jim, my boy? A sea artist, he is. Look you, Bristol, we're bad in need of a navigator. Would you consider signing on the account with us?"

Across Bristol's mind flashed the hardships he had suffered as a British sailor. Scurvy, bad food, gunshot, indifferent medical attention, no shore leave, no pay.

"Sign on?" said Bristol. "Why, of course I'll sign on!"

The midshipman addressed as Jim smiled at him. "That's a good lad. Bryce has been stumbling all about the Caribbean for two months."

"Tell me," said Bristol. "Why did you attack this vessel? It might have blown you out of the water."

"Probably would have if the Lord High Governor hadn't struck his own colors for us."

Mannville's eyes were accusing as he stared at Sir Charles.

"But," continued Bryce, "we needed another vessel besides the one we have. I want to organize a fleet, if I can. This ship looked fine enough and so . . . well, here we are. Avast there, Ricardo, step out here!"

The man so addressed swaggered to the front. His arms hung too far down his sides and, though he was tall, he resembled a barrel in build. His shirt was open at the throat, displaying matted hair. An ugly saber slash divided his face and gave a down cast to one eye.

"Ricardo," said Bryce, "pick your crew. This man is Tom Bristol, a sea artist. He'll stay aboard here with you, and you'll captain this ship."

"Aye, aye, sir," replied Ricardo, running his glance down Bristol's whipcord figure. "Gentleman, eh, Bristol? But that's no matter. We'll get along. I'm what they call pistol-proof, in case we don't."

Bryce looked at the slender midshipman.

"Look now, Jim. You stay aboard here and be my agent. Look alive, the rest of you. Put this scummy British crew off in their boats."

"You aren't going to kill me?" cried Sir Charles.

"I wouldn't dirty my rapier," said Bryce.

The buccaneers attended to the lowering of the boats. The British seamen scrambled into them, thankful to be alive. Bristol moved over to the rail and watched the Lord High Governor pull away.

"And you," cried Sir Charles, catching sight of Bristol, and feeling secure in his boat, "I'll see that you swing from my Execution Dock the next time we meet!"

"I wish you luck!" cried Bristol.

CHAPTER THREE

A Pirate's Penalty

THE days went swiftly for Tom Bristol. To a man who had spent his life in the rigorous merchant marine and had had a taste of the navy, buccaneering was the sailor's dream of Valhalla. Thanks to a steady influx of willing recruits, the pirates were overmanned, so far as handling the ship was concerned.

The decks were scrubbed whiter and cleaner than they had ever been in the service of the King. The sails were repaired and the gear was replaced from ample stores.

Tom Bristol had heard a great deal about buccaneers in his youthful life, but all of it had been bad, and most of it untrue. He saw nothing of cruel orgies. Instead, in spite of the absence of that cat-o'-nine which the navies considered so necessary a part of discipline, he found a peaceful crew, anxious to get along with one another and with their officers.

These men were not the scum of the ports or the sweepings of the sea. They were average seamen who had tired of the filth and abuse suffered in the merchant fleets and the navies. They wanted nothing more than a comfortable life, money to spend, brandy to drink, and a prospect of sometime being able to become planters or merchantmen in their own right.

They owed their fearsome reputation, for the most part,

to cowardly captains who had defended their own valor by besmirching the behavior of the buccaneer, giving that as a reason for struck colors.

Of course they were loud when drunk, but then, what sailor is not? And of course they had quarrels, but these were settled ashore by properly regulated duels.

Justice was administered by a quartermaster who was backed by an impartial jury of the men's own choosing. And if a man were found guilty of theft, cowardice in battle, or perhaps (on rare occasions) murder, he was sentenced to be marooned and was then left on some deserted island with a gun, powder, shot and a bottle of water, to shift for himself thereafter.

In case of the loss of a limb in service, or some other injury, a compensation was forthcoming from the company fund—a provision the navies had not even thought about.

The buccaneers, knowing they could expect nothing less than hanging if caught, went into battle with a determination which could not be matched by men who cared not a whit for their masters.

Bristol, a gentleman once again, was quartered in the Lord High Governor's own cabin. The lockers of the officers had disclosed an abundance of clothes purchased and plundered. And as every buccaneer is allowed a shift of clothing from each prize, Bristol soon turned himself out in a white silk shirt, a red sash and a wide-brimmed hat which had probably been worn by some great *don* in the past. He found sea boots which fitted him and a pair of silver-mounted pistols which were marvels of accuracy, and then began to consider himself a man once more.

Although he was far from being in command, Bristol was an important personage, in that he could do what no other could. He was one of those rarities—a navigator who understood the sun and sextants and stars and charts.

Seated upon the charting table in the great cabin, looking through the large stern ports at the *Terror*'s wake, Bristol listened to the murmur of water along the keel.

Across from him, curled up in a high-backed chair, sat the midshipman known as Jim. Just why a pirate should possess a midshipman was a little puzzling to Bristol, but he asked no questions. The lad was handsome enough, had a low, pleasant voice, and was certainly well educated.

But midshipmen—until a short time before called King's Letter Boys—belonged in the British Navy. They were supposed to be officers in the making, gentlemen born, and the authority they possessed in the King's Navy was something to marvel at. Midshipmen did not have a very wholesome reputation.

But evidently Bryce had thought the idea a good one, and perhaps it was. Though heaven knew, a lad of fifteen didn't belong aboard the *Terror*, or aboard any ship of the day for that matter.

"When do we pick up Bryce?" said Jim.

"Tomorrow afternoon sometime. We'll meet him off Martinico." Bristol smiled. The familiarity with which Jim treated the buccaneer captain was easy and natural. In fact, everything about the lad was that way. The big blue eyes were frank and steady, and the yellow hair, caught up in back, made the eyes seem all the bluer.

"Hope nothing happens to him," said Jim. "He's the only one who keeps Ricardo in leash."

"You don't like Ricardo, do you?"

"No . . . and you don't either. He's captain here because he's pistol-proof, and he gets no end of pleasure out of harrying you, Bristol."

"I suppose you're right. I hadn't noticed that part of it."

"No? Well, he's been telling the men that you are a dainty little thing, and they should be careful of you. They laughed at him, because no matter what you are, you're far from dainty."

"Compliment, Jim?"

"Oh, sure. I mean the adjective is absurd. You're going to have trouble with Ricardo, Bristol. He resents the fact that you wash your ears."

"Pipe down, sailor, he's in the next cabin. He'll hear you."

"Let him listen away," replied Jim, blithely. "I don't believe he'd be so pistol-proof if you took a notion to—"

The cabin door was flung open. Ricardo stooped and entered. Standing erect again, he fixed a colorless eye upon Jim. "Shove off, little one, I want to talk to Bristol."

"I'm sitting right here," said Jim easily.

"The lad's all right," said Bristol.

"He'll be carrying tales to Bryce, if you don't watch yourself, Mister Bristol."

"Oh, I don't think so." Bristol swung his legs and continued to look through the stern ports. The buckles on his sea boots flashed as a ray of sunlight struck them. After a moment he turned to Ricardo. "What's under your hatch?"

Ricardo studied Jim and then shrugged. "Aw, what's the

matter with havin' him hear it? He won't ever see Bryce again anyhow."

Jim's eyes grew suddenly big. Bristol did not move.

"Meaning what?" said Bristol.

"Meaning plenty. Listen, I'm sick and tired of running Bryce's errands for him. One o' these days he'll cut away from us and take all the loot. And we'll swing on some Execution Dock in his place."

"If you're trying to stir me up," said Bristol, "spare yourself the effort. I'm most terribly satisfied with my lot."

"That's because you don't know any better, matey. This Bryce hasn't got the morals of a cockroach."

"Coming from you, that's funny," said Bristol.

"So you don't think he'd let you hang for him?" Ricardo's swinging arms steadied, the elbows bent slowly. Ricardo's thumbs were hooked in his green sash, close to the matchlock dags which were always ready there.

"What's your game?" said Bristol.

"Look here, me bucko, you're a navigator. You can take us any place on the seas. We've got a man-o'-war with seventy guns, and we can lick anything that floats. We've got the goods and florins taken from that last Dutchman. I say let's get out from under and strike out on our own account. The men will all go with me—I've spoken to them about it. They don't owe nothing to Bryce."

"Well, *I* owe something to Bryce. Think that over."

Jim was sitting up straight, white hands gripping the arms of the chair, eyes on Bristol.

Ricardo growled a word as bitter as acid.

"I'm afraid," said Bristol, "that I don't take that from anyone."

"No? Well, my bucko, you'll take it from Ricardo, and like it." A pistol whipped from the green sash.

Before Bristol could gather himself, Jim's small boot lashed out and cracked against Ricardo's knuckles. Ricardo bellowed with rage. His open hand swooped down. The palm cracked loudly against Jim's cheek. Crumpling up, Jim slid into the far corner of the cabin. The jaunty cap fell off and the yellow hair streamed down on either side of the handsome face. The mark of the blow was as red as blood on the white cheek.

Faces were peering in through the door, but Bristol gave them no heed. Both he and Ricardo were staring at Jim. Something about the way the yellow hair fluffed out, something about the way the jacket lay against the throat—

"My God," cried Bristol, "she's a girl!"

Ricardo's other hand was moving. Ricardo's colorless eyes were upon the spot where the bullet would strike Bristol. Men scattered out of the line of fire.

Bristol came off the table like a tenpin. He struck the floor and rolled over. Ricardo's face was wreathed in the smoke which eddied up from Bristol's gun.

Ricardo's eyes went suddenly wide. Bristol was instantly on his feet. The harsh twang of his rapier leaping from its scabbard came almost as an echo to the shot. He lunged. Ricardo parried the blow with his bare hand, and the blade went red. Ricardo's cutlass came out and slashed wildly before him.

Bristol did not think of the niceties of swordplay, nor did he try to avoid Ricardo's rush. His right boot came off the planking, his body swept forward, the boot stamping back. His rapier flickered an instant, and then the flicker died—deep in the chest of Ricardo.

Ricardo's mouth flecked red with froth. He clawed at the blade. Bristol pulled it out. Folding up a little at a time, Ricardo slumped into a dirty pile on the carpet.

Bristol did not look up when the quartermaster spoke.

"Surrender your weapons," said the quartermaster. "You are under arrest of the council."

Bristol tossed pistols and rapier listlessly to the floor. The quartermaster scooped them up and then pointed to the girl. "You'll have to stand charge for that, too."

"For what?" said Bristol, still staring at Ricardo.

"For harboring a woman in disguise aboard this ship. You can bring her, too. We're putting about, and we'll have to place her on shore. Women are too dangerous to keep." The quartermaster withdrew his head and shut the door.

Bristol turned to the girl. Picking her up, he laid her upon the seat beneath the stern ports. Her eyes came open slowly, but it was some seconds before any intelligence came into them.

Then she sat up quickly, only to sink back. She stared at Bristol, who was throwing a sheet over Ricardo. Something seemed to tell her that Bristol knew, for when he came to her side, two big tears welled up in her eyes.

"What . . . what are they going to do with me?"

"Set you ashore."

"But . . . but Bristol! I have no place to go!"

"It's out of my hands. They'll either kill me or maroon me."

The girl turned over and buried her face in her hands.

27

*His rapier flickered an instant, and then the flicker
died—deep in the chest of Ricardo.*

"After everything that's happened these last months, they'll put me ashore!" She was silent for a moment. Then, "And they'll kill the only man I ever respected."

"Look here . . . belay that!" pleaded Bristol, not a little confused. "Who are you?"

"I . . . I was Lady Jane Campbell, lady-in-waiting to Catherine of Braganza, Queen of England."

"Good Lord!" cried Bristol. "You mean . . . Lady Jane Campbell?" He smiled a little and sat down on the table. "The Lord knows women are scarce enough out in this part of the world. Look you, Lady Jane. Do you see that golden goblet over there?"

She nodded, sitting up, wondering what he meant.

"That golden goblet was to be one of your wedding presents. And Sir Charles"—his smile broadened—"and Sir Charles had to leave it behind."

"I know," she replied quietly.

"We were rushing the *Terror* to Nevis to get the Lord High Governor there in time for his wedding—and his bride was aboard the ship which took us."

"I know."

"And you didn't speak up?"

"How could I?" she said quickly.

"How did you get in this mess?"

The tears had stopped. Something like a twinkle came into her blue eyes. "The ship that was bringing me out from England was attacked by Bryce. I had heard so much about pirates that I was afraid I'd come to harm, and when they put off the crew in boats to shift as best they could, I knew my fate at the hands of the crew wouldn't be so good.

"I therefore had but one person to rely upon—myself. I took the uniform from the locker of a midshipman while the fight was in progress and put it on. I knew that a woman could pass for a boy, if the worst came of it.

"Besides, a midshipman is considered an officer. The buccaneers wanted recruits from the crew, and so I stepped out and no one of the original ship's company gave me away. I was the only one to desert them. Bryce thought he needed another watch officer, and thought perhaps he could last long enough to train me.

"I was hard put to it to keep from showing him my ignorance, but he never asked any questions. He told me more than once that I was better off under the Black Ensign than aboard a man-o'-war.

"And then there was something else. I had known Sir Charles Stukely in London, and because I was young and, he thought, timid, he tried to impress me with his manly conduct.

"When he was first ordered out here, he wrote back to Charles II and requested that I be sent to Nevis as his bride. I had to obey my king, but I certainly did not want to arrive in Nevis. And . . . well, here I am."

"They're going to put you ashore," said Bristol. "They'll give you money."

The quartermaster opened the door and entered. A thick-set, red-faced fellow, he had no grace about him. "We're standing off Nevis, Jim. We've stepped a sail in the jolly boat and put some gold in there. You're leaving us."

"But I—"

"You're going ashore," said Bristol. "Look you, quartermaster, what have the council found in my case?"

"You're guilty of fighting aboard and harboring a woman. The penalty is marooning. We're putting you ashore on some island on the Anegada Passage. It's bad to be without an artist, but we'll manage to catch up with Bryce all right. The jolly boat is ready, Jim."

The girl stood up, picked her cap from the floor, and went out to the deck. She was once more a midshipman in appearance. None of the men bore her any ill will. They nodded as she passed through them to the Jacob's ladder.

The jolly boat bobbed in the shelter of the lee. She went down into it and cast off the painter. The craft was whipped astern.

As it passed under the castle ports below the taffrail, she saw that Bristol was standing there, watching her.

"Goodbye, Bristol."

He raised his hand in salute.

She turned quickly and hoisted the single sail. The jolly boat scudded up against the wind toward Nevis.

CHAPTER FOUR

Bristol Finds a Ship

THE *Terror* put about and headed west, with the wind astern and the dying sun turning the spritsails into sheets of beaten gold. The low-hanging clouds along the horizon were pinnacles of flame.

The Anegada Passage—that strip of water which separates the Nevis–St. Kitts group from the Virgin Islands—was, for once, empty of ships. It was the main channel for incoming vessels, in spite of the hazardous sand spits and islands that dot the choppy seas in that region.

Bristol drew a black sea cape about his shoulders and went up on deck. The quartermaster detailed three men to watch him, then went into the great cabin. Presently he came forth, dragging Ricardo.

Hoisting the late captain up on the quarterdeck rail, he dumped the body into the sea. It floated for a moment, black hair sprawling along the surface, and then the foamy wake swallowed it up forever.

The quartermaster approached Bristol. "I suppose we can use the course you already plotted."

"Yes," said Bristol. "When you see Bryce, tell him the truth."

The quartermaster raised himself up on the rail and looked ahead. Squinting his eyes against the red blaze of light on water, he made out a black dot off the larboard.

"Boat's crew!" bellowed the quartermaster. "Man the longboat and prepare to lower!"

Six brawny lads swiftly unlashed the longboat and stood by. The helmsman gave the wheel a spin and the wind went out of the sails. The *Terror* began to roll into the trough. The spars slammed and the canvas cracked, whipping and restless, as though anxious to be gone.

Bristol stepped into the boat. The six followed him. Strong hands began to lower away on the falls. The longboat smacked into the sea and drifted away. The six unshipped their oars and laid them in the double pins in the bulwark. Bristol stood at the tiller.

"Prepare to give way," said Bristol. "Give way all together. Stroke!"

It was the last command he would ever give these fellows—perhaps the last command he would ever give. Looking ahead, across the gay headsilks of the oarsmen, he could see the island rise out of the waves. It was but little better than a sand bar, and there would be neither water nor food upon it.

The *Terror* alternately appeared and disappeared as the longboat swooped from crest to trough and back again. The keen salt spray fanned back to Bristol to stand like pearls on the black broadcloth of the sea cape.

They were going in under the lee of the island. The water was quieter, the surf less severe.

"Oars!" said Bristol.

The sweeps came up. A comber caught in the keel and the boat catapulted in toward the beach. The harsh grind of sand was under them.

Bristol picked up the rifle, the bottle of water and the bag of shot. Walking along the thwarts, he stepped to the sand.

Behind him one of the six took the tiller. They ran through the surf, spray flying up from their churning boots. The longboat drifted out.

"Prepare to give way!" cried the coxswain. "Give way all together! Stroke, stroke, stroke . . ."

Bristol did not look back.

A scraggly line of shrubs lined the beach. He went up to them, looking through the tangle, long and shadowy in the setting sun. His own shadow was a thin black line on the white sand.

Striking out, Bristol skirted the shrubs. The sand was hard to walk in. He was going to make certain that he was alone here, and that there were no springs.

He knew what would happen to him. Although ships passed this point regularly, he would never dare signal them. They would understand only too well that he was a marooned pirate. And if a ship did take him off, he would be promptly hanged from a yardarm.

When his water gave out, that would be the end.

It was almost dark when he had completed the circle. He could see a vague blur of white to the southeast. That would be the *Terror,* sailing to meet Bryce off Martinico. He wondered what Bryce would say—but then, Bryce could say nothing. The law of the pirate was inflexible, and he had been guilty of two offenses.

It mattered nothing that Ricardo had tried to kill him first. If that pistol ball had struck where Ricardo had thought it would strike, then Ricardo would be here instead of Bristol. But Ricardo would be drifting slowly down to Davy Jones' locker by now, accompanied by hungry sharks.

Of course it was barely possible that another pirate would pick him off, but buccaneering activities here in the Caribbean had diminished since the English suppression at Port Royal. The mightier buccaneer captains were across the Isthmus, fighting the *don* in the Pacific.

Bristol sat down and watched the darkness grow thick across the passage. For a while the tip of Nevis still caught the sun, and then that too was gone. Poor Jim! Sir Charles would suspect a lot that wasn't true—and even if he didn't, it would be bad enough to have to live with Sir Charles.

Wrapping the sea cape tight about him, Bristol lounged back on his elbow. The sand was still warm, but it would be cold before morning.

A small sound came to him. The creak of a gaff being run down a mast, accompanied by the fitful whisper of disturbed canvas.

Bristol sat up, tense. Someone was putting in to the beach. His hand tightened upon the flintlock musket. Slowly he cocked the hammer. The muttering monotone of surf obscured all other sounds.

Grating sand brought Bristol to his feet. Someone was dragging at a boat. Boots scuffed up toward the trees.

"Stand!" cried Bristol.

The scuffing stopped.

Bristol raised the gun. "Approach slowly, or I'll fire!"

"Bristol!"

The gun dropped. Bristol tried to pierce the blackness, but could not. The boots were running now, running toward him.

Suddenly a very small person confronted him—a vague whiteness of face and the gleam of a collar.

"For heaven's sake!" cried Bristol. "Jim!"

"Yes, Bristol. I hope you're not angry. I started toward Nevis, but then when I thought of them putting you off on a sand spit, and when I thought of Sir Charles, I turned and followed the *Terror*. I've been standing on and off, waiting for darkness. They couldn't sight me in the sea that's running."

"Angry? Why should I— But look here, Jim—I mean Lady Jane—you shouldn't have done this."

"But I can take you off in the jolly boat. It will sail wherever we want to go in the Caribbean."

"We have no place to go. Port Royal is closed to us, and the Dutch are trying to keep us out of their islands. If we're picked up at sea, it'll mean one thing."

"I can't go back to Nevis, Bristol. It's too much for the jolly boat to work into the wind. It slips sideways."

"Yes, I guess you're right." Bristol went down to the jolly boat and dragged it up on the beach, out of the tide's way. There were several pieces of canvas in it, and he brought them back to the trees.

Spreading them out of the wind, he turned to Lady Jane. "There's your bunk, sailor. I'll keep watch, in case we have other visitors."

She pummeled the sand until she had a hollow to lie in.

That done, she sat up, placed her arms around her knees and said, "We might have a fire. It will make things more cheerful."

"And a cruising man-o'-war would make things more cheerful for us."

"Why so, Bristol?"

"Because they'll know we aren't shipwrecked sailors. Our clothing is too good, and the leather and brass haven't been spoiled by sea water. There is no wreckage strewn along here, and people don't go to sea in jolly boats. They'll know we're pirates."

"I guess you're right. And an English ship would hand us into Nevis immediately."

"God forbid!"

After a little, she lay down on the canvas and drew her own cape tightly about her. Bristol heard her breathing become regular and knew that she slept. Through the rest of the night he sat with his back to the hummock, lost in thought.

Toward morning, with the bitter chill of the tropics upon them, and with the sea as smooth as the surface of a pearl, the girl rose and changed places with him.

Bristol awoke some time later with the tang of frying boucan sharp in the air and the hot midday sun beating mercilessly upon the sand. The rumble of the surf had increased under the whisper of swelling wind.

Jim, sleeves rolled up, shirt collar open, was kneeling by a smokeless fire, holding a pannikin with one hand and a cutlass in the other. Along the cutlass she had alternately placed boucan and slices of a potatolike root she had dug up with the same sword.

When she saw that he was awake, she called out, "Pipe down for mess, sailor!"

Bristol stumbled down to the surf and splashed cool saltwater on his face. It left it sticky, but it revived him. There is nothing more stifling than sleeping late on a hot morning.

Taking his small dirk from his belt, he removed "kabob" from the cutlass. "If I don't cut my tongue out, I'll be all right," said Bristol, grinning.

He had just finished the breakfast when his eye caught sight of a sail. He jumped up and kicked sand over the fire.

"Ship," he said, pointing. "We'd better get back into the trees."

The girl gathered up her jacket and cape and started for the undergrowth. She stopped and looked back. "Bristol! They'll see the jolly boat!"

Bristol nodded. "But that can't be helped."

A scraggly locust tree offered an excellent lookout. Bristol, discarding his white shirt in order to be inconspicuous, swarmed up through the branches. Bracing his sea boots in a junction of limb and trunk, he parted the branches and stared out at the sea.

The vessel was still far away, but Bristol's practiced eye knew her for a Dutch bark of perhaps four hundred tons. There was something shoddy about the set of her sails, and the hull was far from bright. From that, Bristol took her to be a slave ship.

"A blackbirder," he called down to Lady Jane. "She'll pass within a cable length of the place, but she won't do anything." He paused, studying the horizon. "Wait!"

Less than half a league astern of the slave ship came a British cruiser, ship-rigged, with every rag set.

"A man-o'-war!" cried Bristol. "A British man-o'-war trying to catch the blackbirder!"

A small gasp came from the dark jungle below and then leather began to scrape on bark. Presently, Lady Jane's yellow hair appeared below Bristol.

"The slaver's in for it," she said.

The distance between the two vessels was rapidly decreasing. Bristol studied the sea before the Dutchman. A white line of waves, like sharp fangs thrust up from the bottom of the sea, marked a series of shoals. It was quite apparent that the slaver would be forced to hold to her course.

A puff of dirty smoke went up from the man-o'-war's bows. The shot skipped ahead of the Dutchman and landed in a geyser of foam. The detonation reached the island seconds later, like the beat of a bass drum.

It was not that the Englishman objected to the Dutchman's slave-running. The British wanted the slaves and ship for themselves. According to the English way of thinking, England had the slave monopoly in the New World, and this particular blackbirder was an interloper to be properly squashed and looted.

The Dutchman was not without his defiance. A stern chaser spewed smoke and flame back at the man-o'-war. The shot fell short.

Evidently that was all the British wanted. The ship closed in swiftly and yawed. A broadside thundered, drowning the

Englishman in smoke. The Dutchman's masts erupted out of the deck and fell back, a worthless tangle of rubbish.

It required the Englishman several minutes to swing to his course, and the slaver made good use of the time. Stripped of half her motive power, she came about.

It was obvious that the blackbirder would not allow her cargo to be taken, even if she had to destroy herself to prevent it. With a bone in her teeth, she lunged for the shoals.

The man-o'-war's bow chasers hammered out as if iron could prevent the suicide. The Dutchman's bow jumped suddenly, and another mast came down. The ship careened drunkenly, then settled back on her side, with a bad list. Part of her keel was visible.

There was an immediate scurry on the decks. Longboats were lowered into the water. The masts were stepped and the sails hoisted. The crew—some thirty men—shoved off.

Their longboats, having less draft, could easily navigate the shoal. The scudding hulls were battered by spray, but presently all of them emerged unscathed on the far side of the white water, immediately making for the cluster of islands which rose hazily to the west.

The baffled man-o'-war stood on and off for half an hour. It did not want to trust its longboats to the treachery of the shoals. It would be simpler to surprise another Dutchman.

The Englishman disgustedly put about and headed for the Atlantic, in search of easier prey.

Bristol and Lady Jane slid down out of the tree. Bristol put on his shirt.

"Are you thinking what I'm thinking?" said Bristol.

"Maybe."

"I'm thinking that the Englishman did us a good turn. We can get out there in the jolly boat and take what we need by way of provisions and water. That makes things a little rosier, Lady Jim."

"All right. Let's go."

They thrust the jolly boat out into the surf and pushed it through the towering combers into the quieter sea. Bristol set the sail and, tacking crosswind, they bore down upon the shoal water. Lady Jane stood in the prow giving orders which guided them away from clutching disaster.

The stern of the Dutch vessel was in deep water and they had little difficulty in lashing their painter to a trailing line. Bristol went up, hand over hand, to the deck. He pulled the girl up after him.

Bristol wrinkled his nose. "Whew! Slavers aren't exactly perfume chests, are they?"

Lady Jane swallowed hard, a resolute look in her eyes. "But what about the slaves? They're still 'tween decks."

Bristol stopped and looked at the hatches. He knew the roaring mob which might leap out at him if he removed the covers. He knew he would probably have to unchain half of them. And he fully understood the gagging sights which he would face.

He took his pistols from his belt and primed them. Looking about, he saw two serpentines on this afterdeck. They were loaded and a match still sizzled, scorching a brown line along the planks.

Unfastening the lines which held them there, he turned the one-and-a-half-inch muzzles about until they commanded the first hatch. He placed the match in Lady Jane's hand.

"We can't leave them to die down there," he said. "But it's dangerous to try to let them out. If they attempt to charge you, fire these guns, and then—"

"What about you?"

"If they get as far as that hatch, you won't have to worry any more about me."

Bristol strode down through the wreckage of the rigging. With expert fingers he threw back the boards that covered the opening. The stench that leaped out at him was more than sickening. Along with the stench came a low mutter, like that of animals surprised in a den.

Holding a pistol in each hand, Bristol went down the ladder. His eyes became accustomed to the dim interior.

Lying along the planks, in a space which would not allow even a short man to stand, were the slaves. Their manacles clanked as they turned to look at him. They were no more than red-shot eyes in the darkness. Here and there sprawled the dead, still chained.

Out of three hundred slaves shipped from Africa, less than a hundred and fifty had lived to work in the Indies, and this humanity-crammed hull was ample testimony to the reasons. These blacks had not been unchained since they had sailed from Africa, probably months before.

A suffering voice came out of the darkness, uttering words in a foreign language.

"Anyone here speak English?" said Bristol, without hoping to hear an affirmative answer.

He was surprised when the voice changed. "Yes! Yes! You are English?"

"I'm your friend," replied Bristol, "and I'm going to unchain you. But you've got to tell these men that they must not rush. The first man that moves toward me gets a pistol ball through his skull."

"Yes, master. I understand."

Bristol went back up the ladder and nodded to Lady Jane. "I guess it'll be all right. One of them speaks English." He went into the after cabins and came forth in a moment with the chain keys.

Back in the hold he went methodically down the sides of the hot, noisy, smelly interior, trying to hold his breath. The slaves climbed to unsteady feet and crawled up the companionway to the welcome sunshine of the deck. They sprawled there, exhausted by even that small amount of exertion.

Lady Jane watched them with pity. She was surprised at their height. Nubians, they probably were, most of them six feet tall or taller. Although you could see the skeletons in their bodies, at one time they must have had powerful muscles.

They were as black as ebony, except where the chains had worn raw circles about their wrists and ankles. The blood from these wounds dropped slowly, staining the dirty planks.

It was unbelievable that a small ship could hold so many men. One by one they dragged themselves into the sunlight, until there were nearly one hundred and fifty of them on deck.

Lady Jane stayed close by the serpentines, remembering her orders. Some of the blacks were less affected than the others. These went in search of the water casks and came back, ladling out the green-scummed fluid to their fellows. Others found flinty sea biscuits and broke the cases, so that many of the hard disks rolled into the scuppers, to be snatched up by the starved men and devoured with as much appreciation as though they had been cake.

Bristol, his face shiny with sweat, finally came up. "The rest of them are dead," he told Jane.

"The rest of them! Good heavens, Bristol, how many were there?"

"I'm sure I didn't stay long enough to count."

A black dressed in filthy white shorts approached Bristol and saluted. "I am the one who speaks English," he said with meticulous enunciation.

"Why . . . where did you learn that?" exclaimed Jane.

"From the English captives of the Moors. These men, my captain, were all members of an honorable regiment in the service of Badi Abu Daku, King of Sennar in the east of Africa.

"After we had fought for him, and after many of us had died for him, he forgot our pay. And when we reminded him of it, he had us come to his palace. There we were seized, and he sold us to the Arabs who, in turn, sold us to the Dutch. There were once a thousand of us. . . ."

Bristol was tall, but this man was taller by almost a foot. Some of the black's tremendous vitality still remained. His head was well shaped, his brow was high, and his full lips opened to display even, shining teeth. Aside from a white saber slash which ran from his ear to the point of his jaw, he might have been considered handsome.

"What is your name?" asked Jane.

He bowed a little. "I am called Amara, and my rank was a lieutenant—though many years as a slave on the north coast have almost caused me to forget it."

"You know something of the sea, Amara?" said Bristol, his eyes narrow.

Amara bowed again. "I served on the galleys of Tunisia. I was captured by Spaniards, and served on their galleys. I was recaptured and sold to the Dutch. It is only because the use of the galley has become limited in this day of sail that I was allowed to leave them at all.

"Aside from a half-dozen Christians, these men made up the entire galley crews."

Bristol thrust his thumbs into his scarlet sash. He placed his feet wide apart and studied the Nubian's face. "Look you, Amara. If I release you to one of these islands, you will be taken and sold again, to labor and die under the blazing sun."

Amara bowed his head, eyes on the planking. "You freed us, Captain sir, it . . . it is not fitting that you free us only to see us die."

"Right," said Bristol. "You know ships, Amara. What you do not know I can teach you."

"But, Captain sir, you have no ship! This bark is even now beginning to sink under us!"

"I'll have a ship," replied Bristol with a smile which expressed no humor whatever. "Amara, there's a longboat there, left by

46

the Dutch. This bark isn't going to sink for a while. It has a cargo of odds and ends, and it has food and water. Have that longboat manned immediately. God knows, your men should certainly know how to row."

"*Your* men," corrected Amara, beginning to smile.

"Land your men and everything else on that small island there. And watch out for the shoals. Be quick, before a passing ship spots you."

Amara bowed and turned to the men in the waist. He began to bark orders. Dull, listless eyes turned up to him. Life began to flicker there, life and hope and the will to do. . . .

CHAPTER FIVE

Bristol and His Crew Use Strategy

FOUR days passed before the Dutchman slipped off the shoal and disappeared into the blue depths, and a week more had gone by before the blacks had sufficiently recovered to do hard work.

The following days were filled with a tense activity that brought spring into the Nubians' walk and laughter to their lips. They were the offspring of a carefree, fighting people, and even though days spent in Spanish and Barbary galleys had sobered them, they still enjoyed their humor.

The contact with the Christian slaves who had served with them on the galleys had given most of them a smattering of English. Amara had said that his left benchmate was a former British officer. They had passed those long, tedious hours in the bagnios and in port by exchanging languages—a barter that had lasted until the Britisher had fallen under an onslaught of Spanish bullets.

They worked openly, disdaining to shield themselves from passing ships. In fact, it was Bristol's hope that an attack would be launched against him. These blacks were all six feet tall or taller, and the cutlasses they had taken from the Dutchman were like playthings in their strong hands. They scorned pistols and muskets. Steel was their weapon.

The sails of the bark had been ripped up and resewn into very passable tents, and they were all provided with shelter of one kind or another.

Lady Jane, whose quarters had been constructed from the mainsail, retained her identity as Midshipman Jim Campbell. But for the first few days, she was reluctant to go far from her tent. There was something terrifying about these blacks, an undercurrent of bitterness which she felt rather than saw. But as she became used to seeing them and she saw that they had nothing but reverence for her, she grew bolder and went about with Bristol.

At night, when she lay alone in her tent listening to the incessant thunder of the surf, she was sometimes afraid of the power which had been thrown into Bristol's hands. He was tempered steel, physically and mentally, like a long Toledo blade. Into his eyes had come a light which was exciting, but far from reassuring. It was the clear, heady look of one who sees far beyond the horizons.

But when daylight came, that was all forgotten. Bristol was getting them out of that which had promised to be disaster. He treated her with exactly the same deference a shipmaster accords his second mate, and she reveled in it.

Along the beach lay several big logs, and beyond those were clumsy-looking boats, which had been built from the Dutchman's after castle. The logs were burning down the center. Blacks stood by with wet sacking and buckets of sea water to regulate the flames.

These were pirogues in the making. Native canoes which,

when fitted with the outriggers Bristol had seen in the Pacific, would show surprising seaworthiness.

The sunlight of the late afternoon was kind and warm. One of the blacks was singing a wild song at the top of his vocal capacity while another kept time by pounding a plank with a piece of wood.

Amara smiled at Bristol. "He's making it up as he goes along, Captain sir. He says that we will soon be at sea in a beautiful boat."

"I hope he's right," replied Bristol. "Start some of them putting the outriggers on those finished pirogues. We may need them any time."

Amara saluted, "Yes, Captain sir," and went to do the bidding.

"He's a good man," commented Jane, at Bristol's side. "He has taught them all how to handle ship-rigging with that dummy he carved."

"Yes," said Bristol. "He's a good man. And in a fight, I think he'll be even better."

"I'd hate to be standing on a deck, watching those lads come at me."

Up in the locust tree where they had constructed a lookout platform, the sentinel sang out, "Ho! Ship coming!"

Amara roared a question, and when the answer had been flung back, Amara turned to Bristol. "He says it's a Spaniard beating up against the wind, still pretty low on the horizon."

"Good enough," said Bristol. He began to smile. "That ship will be passing the island within two hours—and by that time it will be dark." He swung up into the tree to take a look for himself.

In a half-hour, the entire hull of the Spaniard was visible. The red and gold banner of Castile and León fluttered above a red and gold hull. The vessel was low in the water, outward bound for Spain. Bristol took her to be between six and seven hundred tons.

Coming down, he nodded to Jane. "I know some *dons* that are in for a very bad shock."

"I hope you'll be able to manage it."

"We'll do it right enough. She's tacking within four points of the wind, making less than three knots at best. She's going just slow enough. Amara! Finish off those outriggers, then arm the men!"

In the dusk they launched their boats. It was easily seen where the *don* would pass before she had to go on another tack. Bristol's boats were fastened together in pairs, the line between them being some two hundred feet in length.

It was almost dark before they were in position. They hovered there, watching the running lights swing up on them, keeping the ropes taut. They were drawn up in two lines, one on either side of the Spaniard's course, and the hempen strands barred the vessel's progress.

Of course, the Spaniard would not be expecting attack from shore, and of course, he would not hear the gentle rasp of the lines as they were gathered up by his bows.

Bristol and Jane, in the longboat, watched the masts and sails grow large against the stars. The flutter of canvas, warped to catch the wind at the most extreme angle, the hiss of water

Stories
from the
Golden Age
by
L. Ron Hubbard

Join the Stories from
the Golden Age Book Club Today!

Yes! Sign me up for the Book Club (*check one of the following*) and each month I will receive:

○ One paperback book at $9.95 a month.

○ Or, one unabridged audiobook CD at the cost of $9.95 a month.

Book Club members get FREE SHIPPING and handling (applies to US residents only).

Name   (please print)

If under 18, signature of guardian

Address

City   State   ZIP   Telephone

E-mail

You may sign up by doing any of the following:

1. To pay by credit card go online at www.goldenagestories.com

2. Call toll-free 1-877-842-5299 or fax this card in to 1-323-466-7817

3. Send in this card with a check for the first month payable to Galaxy Press

To get a FREE Stories from the Golden Age catalog check here ○ and mail or fax in this card.

Thank you!

Subscribe today!

And get a FREE gift.

For details, go to www.goldenagestories.com.

For an up-to-date listing of available titles visit www.goldenagestories.com

Stories from the **Golden Age**
by **L. Ron Hubbard**

BUSINESS REPLY MAIL

FIRST-CLASS MAIL PERMIT NO. 75738 LOS ANGELES CA

POSTAGE WILL PAID BY ADDRESSEE

GOLDEN AGE BOOK CLUB
GALAXY PRESS
7051 HOLLYWOOD BLVD
LOS ANGELES CA 90028-9771

spread aside by the plowing bows, and the clatter of a restless spar were all the sounds in the night.

The bow caught the first line, the second, the third. Bristol's boats began to draw silently in, brought near by the ship itself. Black hands were on the hemp, pulling. The other boats were coming back.

Wood grated as bulwark struck bulwark. A head on the deck appeared.

"*¿Quién es?*"

Black hands clutched at the taffrail lines. Black bodies swarmed up. A pistol flamed from the deck.

A shout went up from the ship:

"*¡Filibusteros!*"

The cry was a knife through the night. Men whipped themselves over the rail and to the planking. A cutlass rang out as it struck wood. The helmsman shrieked and ran screaming from his post.

Sailors tumbled out of the hatches. An officer leaped from the rear cabin, pistols in hand. He stood there, paralyzed by the sight that met his gaze. A solid avalanche of black was sweeping down upon him. He fired. A sword hacked him down. The avalanche passed over his body and swept across the deck.

Spaniards cried out. Cutlasses rang as they dropped to the decks. Muskets began to hammer from the forecastle.

Bristol's voice was loud above the tumult, his white shirt rippling in the wind. He dragged a terrified man out of the after cabins.

"Surrender!" cried Bristol.

The captain's ashen face stared up in disbelief. His voice cracked as he cried, *"¡No me mate! ¡El buque es el suyo!"*

A serpentine roared. The shot slammed across the deck. Bristol jerked a whistle from around the captain's throat and blew it three times.

The tumult died. Bristol found a lanthorn and, holding it over his head, walked down into the waist.

The Spanish seamen were crowded against the forecastle bulkhead, eyes wide and white with fear. The blacks stood about, grinning at one another. On the deck lay several bodies, three of them Sennarians.

Bristol located Amara. "See that the weapons are collected."

The Spanish captain had followed Bristol forward. Bristol turned to him now. "There are several boats alongside, *Capitan.* It is an even trade. Ashore on that island you will find a camp of sorts, stocked with food and water. Take your men there and hail the next Spanish ship which passes by."

The captain, who had evidently expected immediate extinction, blinked in the yellow light of the lanthorn. When the truth of the statement came over him, he bowed. *"Gracias, señor.* You are very gallant."

The Spanish crew was herded into the boats, the lines were slashed, and the late captain and his men were lost in the night astern.

"Amara," said Bristol, leaning against the rail, "that was an excellent job. Aboard this ship you'll probably find plenty of clothing and a full larder, as the Spaniard must have restocked before putting to sea. Tell your men to find themselves what they want, and appoint me a watch to handle the sails until morning."

Amara saluted. "Very good, Captain sir."

Bristol turned to Lady Jane. "And I guess this makes full-fledged buccaneers out of us, my lady. That first shot nicked me, thanks to this white shirt. Let's go aft and tie it up."

CHAPTER SIX

A Blow from the British

THE trade wind blew unfailing from the east, brisk enough to press along the most sluggish hull. The Caribbean, marred only by the violence of passing line squalls, remained calm and blue and sparkling. The ring of islands which bounded the sea were green clusters rising from the restless surf.

The Spanish ship, rechristened *Falcon,* had earned herself a reputation. She was a fleet ghost across the trade lanes, to be feared and shunned—not because of excessive brutality, but because of the terrible calmness with which her attacks were planned and carried to completion.

A morning in early July, with the sun at its brassiest, found the *Falcon* scudding in toward the city of Charlotte Amalie, situated on the west of Anegada Passage and just east of Puerto Rico. The *Falcon* had another ship in tow, a French vessel of fifty guns.

The taking of the Frenchman had required but little effort. The colors had been struck after the first broadside. But the captured cargo was comparable to the fight. Cocoa, cotton and indigo had been found under the hatches, and the sterncastle had disgorged nothing more valuable than a sack of Spanish dollars. In Bristol's opinion, it was hardly worth the powder and shot.

Ahead loomed the three ridges behind Charlotte Amalie,

named after the masts of a ship—Foretop, Mizzentop and Maintop. Approaching from the east, the *Falcon* slid past the outer rock formations and glided into the harbor, letting her anchor go with a rumbling snarl of chain.

The city was under Danish control, and commerce was not so good that they could afford to pass up whatever a pirate might wish to bring in. The French ship was still flying her native flag and the Danes had no great love for France. Hence, of course, the French ship acted as Bristol's passport.

Bumboats came out with fruit, unabashed at the presence of a pirate. Blacks held up their wares and looked hopefully at the deck. It was as a distinct surprise to them that the rail should be lined by men of their own race.

But these men were obviously free men. Their gay headsilks and shining belts proved that. Gold coins flickered down into the bumboats, and the fruit was passed on.

Bristol stood on the afterdeck, looking at the French ship, not a little puzzled. "Jim," he said, "I'm sure I don't know what to do with that vessel."

"Sell the cargo," said Jim promptly. "These Danes will buy it for their own shipment, and though they won't give you a twentieth the value, it's better than nothing."

Lady Jane was still dressed as a midshipman, but the quality of the uniform had been bettered. A little more gold lace had been added, and one side of the hat brim was held in place by a blazing ruby. Her neat shoes were dwarfed by the size of the great buckles on the instep. Her long, slender fingers rested on the hilt of a short sword. From her belt protruded the silver inlaid butts of two pistols.

"Bristol," she said, her blue eyes pleading, "can't I go ashore and stretch my legs? I swear it'll be like stepping into a new world, after all this sailing. Besides, there are some things I'd like to buy in those shops."

"It isn't very safe," said Bristol, hesitating.

"Please, Bristol."

"All right. But take a couple of husky lads along with you, and make sure your pistol priming is dry."

Her eyes began to sparkle. She ran into her cabin and Bristol heard her rummaging there for a bag of gold she had been saving for just such a spree.

However, Bristol did not know whether she came out or not. Two men, bulky, and dressed in somber civilian black, came over the rail and waddled aft.

Stopping before Bristol, they bowed. One of them, a little better dressed than the other, said, "I am Jersen, a cargo broker, Captain Bristol. I see that the French have graciously presented you with a prize. How much will you take for the cargo?"

"I'll have to check it over first," replied Bristol.

"Our lighters are being sculled out even now, Captain," said the other. "You can check it into them."

"We are the only cargo brokers here," added Jersen.

Bristol looked at his main deck. Amara was sitting against a mast, cleaning his guns. The others on deck all wore their cutlasses.

"The bargain will be quite fair," said Bristol, jerking his thumb at his crew.

Jersen became a little pale. "Oh, yes, Captain Bristol. Quite fair indeed."

The other man quickly changed the subject. "Have your slaves go over and begin shifting the goods," he said.

Bristol looked surprised. "My slaves?"

"Why . . . why, yes," the Dane replied, certain that he had somehow made an error, but not quite certain just what error it had been. "These men about your deck."

"You mean my crew," replied Bristol, an undercurrent of anger in his voice. "These men are free men, not slaves. I don't happen to be of your stamp, gentlemen. When I take lives I use a rapier, not the whipping post and starvation, and yet I am a pirate, while you and your brothers are supposed to be civilized beings."

"No offense," said Jersen quickly.

"These men," said Bristol, "are sailing with me on the account. When they tire of this life, they can go back to Africa with money enough to buy and sell their rulers."

"You mean," gasped Jersen, "that you consider them as equals?"

"More than a naval captain considers *his* men as equals. And I might remark," said Bristol with a quiet smile, "that I would rather sail with this crew than one of your breed. Come, let's get at the cargo."

Longshoremen from the city did the work, under the watchful eyes of Amara and the pirate quartermasters. Bristol watched the proceedings, checking with a manifest he had found among the French ship's papers.

In the middle of the afternoon, a small sloop ran out from the ramshackle wharves and scudded by the *Falcon,* giving the pirate a wide berth. Bristol was amused and called it to Amara's attention. A few hours later he was to remember the incident with great bitterness.

Toward evening, when all the cargo had been shifted to the lighters and payment had been made, Bristol went back to the *Falcon*. As he came over the side, the black quartermaster in charge of the deck watch saluted with military precision.

Bristol looked aft. "Where is Jim?"

The black shook his head. "I have not seen him, Captain sir. Perhaps he has found the city too interesting."

Bristol frowned and went to the cabins, expecting to find that Lady Jane had returned unseen by the watch. But the cabins were empty.

Angrily, Bristol came up and glared at the city, which was hazy in the dusk. The rows of white houses gave him no answer. He took up a notch in his sword belt and looked to his pistol priming.

"Amara!" he shouted. "Lay aft with six men! We're going ashore to find the second officer!"

Bristol was deeply troubled. If anything happened to Jim—

They slid down into a longboat. Bending their supple backs to the task, the oarsmen sent the craft flying across the quiet harbor.

Bristol guided it expertly alongside a stone pier and jumped up to the dock. He detailed a man to wait with the boat and then, with Amara and the other five following him, he strode toward the brightest street.

Men drew back into doorways as he passed. They stepped

off the sidewalks, out of his way. Behind him came a mutter of speculation.

Ship lanthorns spread great patches of yellow light before the shadowy entrances. Bristol passed under them, his eyes raking the shadows. Behind him, as straight as masts, came the powerful blacks.

Charlotte Amalie had few streets to offer, but these were twisting, and masked in shadow. Amara struck fire into one of the lanthorns after they had made the round of the main thoroughfares.

"I shall look in the alleys," said Amara. "Perhaps something has happened to Mister Campbell, sir. He had a bag of gold when he went off the vessel."

"Then scatter out," rapped Bristol. With the passing of time he had become very worried. He was not certain of the friendliness of this town, but he did not think that anyone here would be foolish enough to provoke the anger of a heavily armed ship.

A few minutes later, Amara came out of a narrow alley. He beckoned to Bristol. Following him, Bristol went deep into the narrow, unpaved street.

Amara held up the lanthorn. Ahead of them, sprawled in the refuse, was a Sennarian. His headsilk was darkly splotched on one side. The cutlass he clutched in his stiffened fingers was stained halfway to the hilt.

"This man was with Mister Campbell," said Amara simply.

A mutter came from the sailors. "By heaven," cried Bristol, "I'll smash this town into a heap of ashes!"

He strode toward the docks, boots ringing out on the stone,

sword belt jangling. His mouth was hard and thin, and in his eyes glittered a cold, deadly anger.

Amara caught up with him, advanced a little before him and touched fingers to cap. "Sir, the bombardment might harm Mister Campbell. Perhaps they are holding him as hostage."

Bristol stopped and swallowed hard. He was unable to understand just why he had lost his head so completely. His only wish was to wreak revenge upon this city. He wanted to rip it bodily apart and set a torch to the shambles.

He nodded. "Thank you, Amara."

Turning, he headed for the largest tavern along the waterfront. From the open doors came a babble of voices and the clink of glasses. Bristol strode in.

Eyes jerked around to him. A silence started at the entrance and swept back through the building. Rum stopped halfway to open mouths.

Bristol raked them with his glance. His voice was as brittle as breaking glass. "My second officer is missing in this city. If I do not get him back in an hour, I'll stand off and blow your island apart."

The silence deepened and became electric. A man finally detached himself from a table and walked haltingly toward Bristol. He was plainly dressed, evidently an official of the city.

"I . . . I know nothing about this, Captain Bristol. But until this afternoon, an English sloop lay in along a wharf. The English left me this paper for posting."

Bristol jerked the slip from his hand, read it swiftly.

Know all ye!

His Majesty Charles II of England has this day placed a price upon the head of one Captain Thomas Bristol, late deserter from the Royal Navy, now become an infamous pirate preying upon lawful shipping in Caribbean waters. For the head of this man will be paid to the sum of Pounds Gold Two Hundred. For the second officer of the *Falcon*, wanted only alive, will be paid an additional Pounds Gold Two Hundred when delivered up to the Lord High Governor of Nevis, Sir Charles Stukely.

Proclamation issued this
First Day of July in the Year of Our Lord 1681
at the Palace of the Lord High Governor of Nevis,
Sir Charles Stukely

Bristol relaxed a little. His laugh was as sharp as the ring of a cutlass on steel. "Any of you gentlemen wish to collect this two hundred pounds?"

No one moved. Bristol thrust the paper into his red sash and spun on his heel. Amara shoved his pistols back into his belt and fell in alongside of Bristol.

They dropped into the longboat, placing the dead man in the bows for burial at sea, and shoved off for the *Falcon*, whose lights sent long yellow streamers across the silent black water.

"Weigh anchor!" cried Bristol, when he reached the deck. "We're off for Nevis!"

CHAPTER SEVEN

Black Ensign Against
Red and White

NEVIS stands out of the sea like an inverted cone, rising more than three thousand feet above the ringing sparkle of white surf. Bristol gave the visible upper half a disgusted study. The *Falcon* was making slow enough progress up against the wind, and now it appeared that her progress would be wiped out completely.

A British man-o'-war, a seventy-four gunner, from outward appearances, was boiling down the waves with the wind abeam. The white and red naval ensign whipped defiantly from the truck, and the taut sails presented a solid pyramid of white.

The *Falcon* was more than a match for the man-o'-war, but the English ship would carry nothing by way of loot, and besides, Bristol had other things in mind.

The well-trained black gunners were stacking pikes and cutlasses, and making certain that the "pieces of seven" cannon were ready. They worked swiftly and smoothly, showing neither excitement nor fear. But Bristol knew that an engagement would weaken him considerably, and even before the first broadside rang out, he had altered his plans.

He would have to go ashore and try to smuggle Lady Jane out of Charlestown. As much as he would have liked to give

Sir Charles a lesson, Bristol was certain that he would have to forgo the pleasure.

A quartermaster sent a wad of dark bunting rocketing up the trucks. It burst there into the Black Ensign.

"Port a bit," said Bristol to the helmsman.

The *Falcon* swerved a little to meet the charging man-o'-war. In the waist, the black gun captains were blowing on their sputtering matches, ready to ignite the touchholes.

Bristol tossed off his sea cape and loosened his rapier in its scabbard. The wind whipped against the wide brim of his rakish hat, raising it in front. Bristol's lean face was impassive, although he recognized this ship to be the *Terror*. If the *Terror* was back in British hands, then what of Bryce?

Up the British truck went a set of signal flags. The other ship was so close aboard that Bristol needed no glass to read them. The two-pennant combination, bright and whipping against the blue sky, read "Come alongside."

"Stand ready with your matches!" roared Bristol to the gunners. "Port again," he told the helm.

The man-o'-war luffed and coasted nearer, sails fluttering. The *Falcon* went cautiously toward her. After a moment, less than twenty feet separated the two vessels.

"Ahoy, *Falcon*!" cried Lieutenant Ewell from the man-o'-war's rail. "I call upon you to surrender!"

Bristol's mouth twisted into a hard smile. "My broadsides are ready. If you have anything to say to me, say it!"

Lieutenant Ewell glanced back at the man who stood behind him—Captain Mannville. Then he shouted through cupped hands, "Bryce is a prisoner at Charlestown. If you surrender, you will be granted the King's clemency."

Bristol was shaken. If Bryce had been taken, then he would probably have to fight additional ships in the harbor. And he would have to attack, fortifications or no fortifications. He owed that to Bryce.

"My broadsides are ready!" cried Bristol. "I'll give you ten minutes to clear away from me."

On the other deck Captain Mannville raised his hand and brought it down in a swift jerk. The British gun captains applied their matches and scampered away from their cannon. A cloud of smoke and sparks leaped up from the touchholes.

"Fire!" snapped Bristol.

Ducking into the protection of the rail, the black crew watched their gunners whip their own matches into place.

The man-o'-war's broadside was deafening. A cloud of bitter smoke shot out, covering up the *Falcon*. Iron smashed into the pirate's hull. Splinters geysered, as deadly as bullets.

The *Falcon*'s own guns exploded as one. The rail was high and the hail of twenty-eight-pound shot ripped great holes in the man-o'-war's rigging, made havoc of the decks. Bristol saw his helmsman go down and snatched at the spinning spokes. The *Falcon*, shrouded in the greasy powder fog, lunged for the Britisher's rail.

Both ships jarred under the impact of bulwarks.

"Boarders away!" bellowed Bristol.

Blacks swept out of the waist, over the rail, and aboard the man-o'-war. Cutlasses flashed. Muskets hammered from the rigging. Gun crews snatched up weapons and dashed into the fight.

Bristol, rapier in hand, went over the side of the *Falcon* and sprinted along the *Terror*'s rail like a tightrope walker. Men hacked at him from below. His rapier was a darting snake's tongue, everywhere at once. Bristol pressed on aft.

Mannville stood on the quarterdeck, pistols in hand. He saw Bristol. The pistols came up. Bristol leaped down to the deck. The shot whistled over his head. Springing up again, he tried to press Mannville back against the sterncastle.

Mannville, his face quite pale, dropped back, trying to avoid the rapier point that menaced him.

"Strike your colors!" Bristol ordered.

The blue and white ensign with its red cross of Saint George slid swiftly down to the deck. Bristol blew three shrill blasts on his boatswain's pipe. The tumult died in the waist.

Eight of Bristol's blacks were stretched on the man-o'-war's planking. Others clutched wounded arms and heads, grimly determined not to groan. Of the man-o'-war's crew, more than ten were dead.

"Now," said Bristol in a very calm voice, "what were you saying before you forgot yourself and fired before you had ended your truce?"

"One of these fine days," said Mannville, "you'll meet your match, Bristol."

"*Captain* Bristol to you. Now what happened to Bryce?"

Ewell hesitated a moment and then said, "He was surprised off Martinico by a British squadron a few weeks ago, and both his ships were taken to Charlestown. Bryce will stand on Execution Dock within a week—and good riddance."

"Watch your tongue!" said Bristol curtly. "Those blacks know you fired out of turn. They'd like nothing better than to string you up by your thumbs and beat you with that cat-o'-nine over there."

Ewell sagged, incredulous. "But . . . but you wouldn't! You're not a barbarian, you're a gentleman! What of the white prestige?"

"I'm glad you found out I was a gentleman. Quick, Ewell! How many ships are there in Charlestown harbor, and how many guns at the fort?"

"A man-o'-war in the harbor. Bryce's ships have not been manned because of"—Ewell gave a despairing look at Mannville, then at the cat-o'-nine—"because we're short-handed there. But the fort batteries, Captain Bristol, are armed with thirty eight-thousand-pound cannon." A bit of belated bravado came into his voice. "That's one point you'll never pass. Those 'pieces of eight' will sink you!"

"Ah, well," said Bristol, "it must be chanced. Amara! Get these prisoners under the hatch."

CHAPTER EIGHT

Battle Breaks in the Harbor

IN the solemn grayness of early morning, Bristol's prize, the *Terror*, entered the narrows that led to the inner harbor. In tow was the *Falcon*, flags and sails drooping, Amara in charge. The mist hung close to the water, almost obscuring both vessels. The breeze was barely enough to move the man-o'-war along.

From the deck of the *Terror*, Bristol saw the high walls of the stone fort rising sheer above them. Gaping black eyes looked down—the snouts of the "pieces of eight"—ready to deal violence to anyone who took it upon himself to attack the city of Charlestown.

Bristol had chosen his moment well. He did not have to display his flag, because this was before the morning colors, nor did he have to announce himself to the fort. In spite of the mist, it was light enough for the sentries to identify the *Terror* as British.

A voice came down from the battlements: "Ahoy, Mannville! Congratulations on your prize!"

Bristol stood tense at the rail. He could not reply to the officer up there. Close inspection would cause them to discover the black gunners who stood in the waist, ready at the British guns. Looking back, Bristol saw no movement aboard the *Falcon*. He knew men were waiting and ready there.

They slid slowly past the Point, into the quieter harbor. Evidently the officer had expected no answer. The dead, languid silence of the city was unbroken. If only this fog would hold until they could come within half a cable length of the docks!

The shadowy, silent hulk of the station ship loomed before them. Bristol coasted by. He would have to reef his sails, and that would necessitate sending his blacks up into the rigging.

"All hands aloft," said Bristol, as quietly as he could. If only this fog . . .

The blacks swarmed up the shrouds. Canvas fluttered and billowed under the freshening breeze. A ray of sunlight pierced through and sparkled on the water, as though someone had jerked a gray curtain from the world.

In less than half a minute the harbor was clear and blue. Red-roofed buildings were thrown into sharp relief. The man-o'-war at anchor, less than a pistol shot away, was visible to her last peg.

Blacks came down in a swift rush, trying to get out of sight before they were noticed.

"Ahoy, Mannville!" cried an officer on the other deck. "What— Quarters! All hands on deck! Man the guns!"

"He's seen us!" muttered Bristol. Looking back, he saw that the *Falcon* still cruised under the pressure on her mainsail and sprit.

Bristol yanked on the truck halyards. The bunting raced to the peak and whipped out to display the Black Ensign. Amara's men, on the *Falcon*, went racing to their guns.

The anchored British man-o'-war was in perfect firing

position. Her guns slammed back. Smoke raced across the water. Grapeshot rapped like hail on the hull of the *Terror*.

"Fire!" roared Bristol.

The starboard batteries crashed out, all three decks simultaneously. The Britisher reeled under the blow.

"Come about!" cried Bristol to the helm. The *Terror* executed a swift jibe. Her port batteries fired across the Britisher's decks.

The Britisher, still at anchor, tried valiantly to turn. And then it became apparent that Ewell had lied. Bryce's old ship surged away from her anchorage, slipping her hawser, and plunged out toward the *Falcon*. She was evidently well manned.

But Amara had learned well under Bristol's tutelage. The *Falcon* swerved to meet the rush. Her starboard batteries crashed. The Britisher was instantly deluged by a hail of its own spars and rigging.

Bristol ran his ship in close to her. His port guns were ready to let drive. His black gunners held their matches in steady hands, blowing on the hemp to keep the fire going.

"Fire!" cried Bristol.

Three rows of black snouts leaped out of sight, replaced instantly by a slashing horizontal column of smoke. The Britisher was swallowed up in the stinging smoke. Bristol's deafened ears caught a string of commands on the other's deck. A trumpet shrilled.

Bristol's vessel slipped away. He was running no chance of being boarded. He was undermanned. The Britisher could have swamped him in a moment, had the Britisher only known it.

The next glimpse Bristol caught of the man-o'-war, it was hurling spray from its bows, sails taut in the quickening wind, heading for the outer harbor. For a moment, Bristol thought the other was running away, and then he understood. The man-o'-war would cruise out there, lying in wait for the pirates.

It came over Bristol in that instant that he was trapped. The *Terror* and the *Falcon* could never pass through the narrows, and they did not possess enough men to storm the fort. And when they reached the sea, the waiting British man-o'-war would pounce upon them, board them, and wipe out the remainder of the pirates.

There was only one answer to that. He'd have to get up to the palace and put the fear of the devil into Sir Charles Stukely. But without a large landing party, that appeared to be impossible.

The *Terror* keeled suddenly. A round shot from the fort smashed against her rail, demolishing it.

Bristol stared at the shore. He could see men running back and forth, barricading themselves. Without a force of a hundred men, it would be impossible to effect a landing—and even then, the odds would be two to one.

The *Terror* shook again. The batteries ashore were getting the range, and although it was inconceivable that a round shot could pierce a stout oak hull, Bristol detected a sluggish lurch.

A man named Funj ran up through the smoke, shouting to Bristol, "The starboard ports are filling up! The 'tween-deck cannon are loose!"

Harassing shot came from the fort. Amara's *Falcon* still

cruised nimbly, returning a steady but ineffectual fire. The *Terror* plowed toward the white sand, going down an inch for every foot gained ahead.

"Get down!" ordered Bristol, keeping his own feet. "Scatter about, and get your cutlasses and pikes! We'll have to wipe out the men on shore!"

The soldiers ashore grew bolder. They leaped into the open, waving their guns, running toward the spot where the ship would ground.

Bristol saw with surprise that most of these men were black. Was it possible that the planters had sent forth their slaves to do their fighting for them? Did Sir Charles think the English regulars too good to risk their necks? Disgust welled up in Bristol—disgust for a feudal system that had come down from the medieval days, when men were mere beasts of burden.

The sinking *Terror* came within a hundred feet of the sand. Suddenly the head slumped. The entire ship jerked over in a heavy list. Thrown bodily into the port scuppers, the blacks fought to keep their balance. Bristol held his breath, hoping that the water was too shallow for them to sink all the way under.

The ship stopped completely, leaving fifty feet of water between its prow and the beach.

"Landing party away!" shouted Bristol.

Whipping out his own rapier, he plunged forward, over the forecastle deck. In a clean dive he swooped down into the sea. The blacks came after him like an avalanche. Musket balls from shore sent long white streamers through the water.

"Landing party away!" shouted Bristol.
Whipping out his own rapier, he plunged forward,
over the forecastle deck.

The savage cry of the pirates swelled up. Bodies glistening with water, they charged, wet silks clinging tight to their bodies. A black from shore tried to catch Bristol's rapier on his musket barrel. The point slid off with a clang and plunged into the black throat.

A high wall, topped by embrasures, was at one hand. Bristol looked at it, took it to be an arsenal. Waving his rapier for his men to follow, he sprinted for the open gate. He could at least hold out in the place.

Inside the court, Bristol did not pause. He saw a tier of doors opening. Men sprang at him. His blacks stopped and stood their ground. The sunlight was shattered by swinging, stained blades.

Behind them, a sailor barred the gate.

Musket balls whined through the court. Soldiers were sniping from adjoining roofs.

A strident voice roared, "Bristol! For God's sake, man, let me out of here!"

Bristol jerked his head around, dashing the blood from his eyes so that he could see. "Bryce!"

The pirate captain was beating with bare fists upon the door, shouting through the bars. This, then, was the jail. No wonder it had looked like a fort!

An officer was crumpled at the bottom of a flight of stairs. Bristol whipped the man over and found a ring of keys. He ran to the cells and quickly opened the locks. Bryce rushed out, eyes wild, teeth clenched.

"We'll whip them now, Bristol! By the Lord, I've waited weeks for this chance!"

"But I've only got fifty men!"

"The hell you have! I've got three hundred underground in this building!"

Above the roar of cannon and the bark of muskets, Bristol heard the muted cries of men. He thrust the keys at Bryce. "Open the doors. Get them out here!"

A hammering came from the gate. Funj saluted and said, "They're using a battering ram, sir. The gates are caving in."

Bristol looked into the guardroom. Long boxes were scattered about on the floor, like coffins ready for their dead. On the lid of one was marked "To the Governor General of Santo Domingo, New Spain."

"Loot from a *don*," cried Bristol. He kicked the cover from one and found that it contained cavalry sabers which, though greased and gummy, would serve quite well.

Bristol and Funj threw the saber cases bodily out into the court. The blades scattered out of the broken boxes and were at once snatched up by eager hands.

The gate began to go. In a thunder of splinters, it came down. A wave of soldiers, black and white, spilled across the shattered boards into the courtyard.

The pirates howled with glee. Sabers aloft, they bore down upon the soldiers like iron shot from a broadside. It was too late for the men in the gate to go back. They stopped, tried to raise their weapons to defend themselves. The mad tide crushed them down, ground them to the pavement, and went on and through the gate into the street.

Abruptly the defenders broke into scattered segments. They

took to their legs, throwing away their guns and equipment. The pirates started to follow.

"Avast!" roared Bristol. "To the palace! There's our game!"

The yelling mob swept up through the streets toward the white building on the hill. A cannon at the palace gates rapped, carved a straight line through the attackers. The glinting snout of the gun protruded through the bars of the heavy locked gate. The men at the piece crammed in a second load of powder and canister.

Bristol reached the walls. Two of his blacks were with him.

"Up!" he cried.

The blacks grasped his waist and threw him to the top of the wall. The gun crew stared an instant. An officer reached for his pistol. Bristol launched himself. His rapier grated on bone. The crew at the gate whirled on him, drawing their swords.

A cry came from the wall. Pirates, boosted by their fellows, soared over and dropped into the court. The gun crew threw away their swords and ran.

Bristol looked at the front entrance of the palace. The doors were heavy oak, carved in a coat of arms. He tested the latch. It was securely barred within.

"The cannon!" snapped Bristol.

A half-dozen of his black gunners quickly completed the job of loading. They pulled at the carriage. The touchhole shot out sparks. Bristol leaped to one side. The round shot slammed through the lock. The doors, emerging from the smoke, were shattered.

Accompanied only by Bryce and a few of the blacks, Bristol strode toward a second set of doors. Their boot heels rang loudly on the black polished floor, their sword chains clanked.

The doors opened at a touch to disclose an ornately furnished room. Sir Charles Stukely sat behind his desk, his eyes large and fishy with surprise and terror. He was dressed in a bright blue coat, and gems sparkled on his pudgy fingers.

"C-Captain Bristol!" said Sir Charles hoarsely.

"Aye, Captain Bristol. Weren't you expecting me?"

"Ah . . . ah yes, of course I was. I—"

"I see you're dressed like a bridegroom, Sir Charles. Why didn't you send me an invitation to the wedding?"

"I . . . ah, of course, Captain Bristol, I should like to have you at . . ." Sir Charles gulped audibly, suddenly realizing that he was being baited, recovering with an effort control over his wits. Bristol went on:

"But I came, anyway, and held my own wedding party. Thank you for the reception your slaves and soldiers gave us. It was greatly appreciated. But," he added reprovingly, "I thought the gentlemen of Old England did their own receiving. I see now that I was wrong. They use their bondmen and slaves, and fight their sea battles with the pickings of a press gang. Well, no matter. When does the wedding take place?"

"Er . . . this after . . ."

"Ah, well, this afternoon. Then I'm just in time." Bristol shifted his weight easily and the sea boots dripped saltwater into a fresh puddle. The trickle of red down his cheek had reached his collar, staining the once white shirt. "Where is the bride?"

"What are you—you going to do with me?" chattered Sir Charles.

Bristol shrugged pleasantly. "Oh, nothing much." He reached into his rumpled sash and brought forth a snaky, writhing object which he flicked casually enough.

"The . . . the cat-o'-nine-tails!" cried Sir Charles.

"Then the idea affects you unfavorably? I thought a man of your stout heart, a man who can stand on a deck and cry 'Give him a hundred lashes!' would show a little more courage under the same sentence."

"But it's *death*!"

"So you knew that it was death!" Bristol regarded the flabby folds of pasty white which made up Sir Charles' face. Bristol's mouth curled a little in disgust. "Strip him!" he said curtly to his blacks.

The sailors, grinning, fell upon Sir Charles and jerked him to his feet. While they were stripping him to the waist, Bristol stepped to the balcony and signaled the *Falcon* with his waving sash. The *Falcon* drew off from the fort to the extreme range.

Sir Charles' body was white and fat. The blacks held his arms. Bristol made the cat-o'-nine swish warningly on the floor. It came up and cracked down upon the cringing Sir Charles. The Lord High Governor screamed out, although the lash could not have hurt him. His voice was broken:

"Bristol! I'll do anything you ask! Anything!"

Bristol stood in pretended indecision. Then he let the cat-o'-nine fall to the floor. "Put on your shirt."

Sir Charles slipped quickly into the broadcloth and slumped back at his desk, his face as gray as death.

A side door of the room opened slowly. Bryce stood up straight, an amazed look flashing across his hard face. The blacks glanced up and then straightened.

Lady Jane Campbell stood in the entrance. About her were great billows of white shimmering satin, drawn in tight to her waist. A cap of pearls rested upon her yellow hair and a corsage of rare orchids matched the delicate beauty of her face. She stepped hesitantly forward, very tense. Then she ran forward.

"Bristol!" she cried.

He held her away from him, gazing at her. The orchids had been crushed against him and one of her cheeks was smudged by the blackness of his own.

"Bristol," she said, "look in the papers on the desk for the letters he took from me on my arrival here."

"Papers!"

"Yes. The papers I went ashore to get at Charlotte Amalie. The papers I sent to England for. The papers that cost me a bag of gold."

Sir Charles made an effort to stop Bristol's hands. He was brushed aside, and Bristol rifled through the stacks of documents. Presently he brought forth a packet that was sealed by the ring signet of Charles II, King of England.

Breaking the seal, Bristol read, "'By Royal Decree I hereby grant full pardon for all the piracies of Captain Thomas

Bristol, and by reason of his possible benefit to the Crown, I hereby enclose a commission as Commodore in the Royal Navy.'

"But . . ." said Bristol, "but, Jim, how did you get this?"

"You have forgotten," she replied gently, "that I was lady-in-waiting to Catherine of Braganza, Queen of England. I sent for that months ago, and the bearer was to meet me in Charlotte Amalie."

A little stunned, Bristol gripped the edge of the desk, staring at the seals of the commission. Then he drew in a long breath and exhaled it in a sigh. In a moment he stood up straight, all business.

"Sir Charles," said Bristol, "can you write?"

"Why, of course I—"

"Then write, quickly. 'To His Majesty Charles II, London, England. Because of the rigors of this climate, and with all apology for the abruptness of this decision, I, Sir Charles Stukely, your humble subject, regret that I must resign the office of Lord High Governor of Nevis.'"

"Wait!" cried Sir Charles. "You can't—"

Bristol flashed the seals on the commission. "See that, Stukely? That means that I rank every other British naval officer in the Caribbean Sea. In case you have forgotten, there is a war in progress for the possession of these islands. This is a military necessity."

"Yes," replied Sir Charles meekly.

"Then proceed. '—that I must resign the office of Lord High Governor of Nevis.' Got that? All right. 'Hoping for your Royal pardon in this matter, I am leaving aboard a man-o'-war immediately for Jamaica, where I shall take passage on a merchantman. I am convinced that I owe this to my health and well-being. In command of the garrisons, and as temporary governor of the island, I am leaving Thomas Bristol, Commodore, Royal Navy.

"'Your honorable and most obedient servant, Sir Charles Stukely.' I will mail that letter for you. You might wish to change it en route. In that event, the King might hear of this little skirmish out here. And so, Sir Charles, I'll save you the price of postage."

"What about me?" said Bryce, puzzled. "I'm still a pirate."

"Never mind," Bristol said. "I'll issue you special privateering papers, commissioning you to prey upon Spanish commerce and you can leave for the Pacific, where you always wanted to be anyway."

Bristol turned to Sir Charles, smiled at him, and then walked over to Lady Jane.

"My lady," said Bristol, "you recently came to Nevis with the object of marrying the Lord High Governor. It happens at this time, due to the fortunes of the sea, that I am that person. May I, in all humbleness, ask your hand?"

Her answer was low and husky. "Of course, Bristol."

Bristol straightened, and his smile broke into a gay laugh. He whirled on Bryce. "Avast, you lubber! Send those pirates of yours and my crew into the barracks to clean themselves up. And spread the news through the town and the fort, and to the waiting man-o'-war, that the Lord High Governor invites them all to his wedding."

Story Preview

Story Preview

NOW that you've just ventured through one of the captivating tales in the Stories from the Golden Age collection by L. Ron Hubbard, turn the page and enjoy a preview of *Twenty Fathoms Down*. Join diver Hawk Ridley as he battles against a rival salvage crew that will stop at nothing to steal the unimaginable wealth he's found in the depths of the Caribbean Sea. A rollicking adventure, complicated only by a beautiful stowaway. . . .

Twenty Fathoms Down

H AWK RIDLEY picked up the yellow sheets of parchment, folded them into a compact bundle, and placed the whole in the pouch that hung around his neck. "I'll take charge of these things now that we're under weigh," he said. "If they're worth a hundred thousand dollars to Chuck Mercer, they're worth ten times that to us."

Captain Steve Gregory gave the receding lights of New York a parting squint and then glanced out across the rain-spattered decks of the *Stingaree*.

"Judging from past events," he remarked, "I'd say those things are a good death warrant. Believe me, Hawk, I look for plenty of trouble down off Haiti. It's my guess that that old galleon has more than a few million in gold aboard her."

Hawk's lean, bronzed face relaxed in a grin and he shifted his lanky weight against the charting table. Youth and the anticipation of adventure made his sea blue eyes sparkle. The captain looked at his chief and then his own round, sunburned face also relaxed.

"Doesn't worry you much, does it, Hawk?" continued Gregory. "You'd think that a diver like you would be having the shakes. Why, boy, you don't even know what Mercer may have in store for us! Twenty fathoms down is pretty darn—"

"Stokey Watts and I will take care of twenty fathoms,"

Hawk interrupted. "All you've got to do is to get this tub of rust down into the Windward Passage off Haiti. We'll do the rest. We're going to get that treasure this time, Greg, and don't you forget it!"

Gregory laughed suddenly. "Anyway, you sure gave Al Mercer a send-off! I'll be a long time forgetting the way that boy took the dive when you threw him down the gangway tonight!"

"He did look funny, didn't he?" agreed Hawk. "But any time anybody points a gun at me and demands that I hand over anything, I'm apt to get cross. They've tried to buy these charts, then steal them, and then to put us out of commission. Lord only knows what they'll do next."

The *Stingaree's* captain was suddenly sober. "Yes, the Lord only knows. I'm looking for trouble, Hawk. Not that I want it, but I know it's coming. Al and Chuck made enough sly remarks as to what would happen if we so much as weighed anchor to go after that bullion."

Hawk looked out across the sea as though his keen eyes could pierce the rain-drenched dark and see the coast which was their goal.

"They're certainly after us," he said.

Well, it was enough that the salvage ship was at last putting out for the West Indies with her diving equipment and competent crew. The sailing had been delayed day by day for two weeks. Minor troubles, just serious enough to rasp on the men's nerves, had occurred with relentless regularity, and the blame had been laid—not without reason—at the door of Ocean Salvage, a rival firm managed by Chuck and Al Mercer.

The bridge itself gave enough indication that trouble of one sort or another was anticipated. Racks of rifles climbed up the after side of the chart room, and ammunition boxes were carefully stowed so as to be handy, yet out of the way.

Even the engines below decks seemed to throb in a subdued, cautious key, as though they, too, sensed danger. The rain, whispering against the steel plates of the decks, added to the feeling of danger ahead.

But though Hawk Ridley and Gregory were keyed up against surprise, the seeming apparition that appeared in the open doorway gave them a shock. For, of all things they expected to see on a salvage ship, a slender, lovely girl in a bedraggled wedding dress was the last.

To find out more about *Twenty Fathoms Down* and how you can obtain your copy, go to www.goldenagestories.com.

Glossary

STORIES FROM THE GOLDEN AGE *reflect the words and expressions used in the 1930s and 1940s, adding unique flavor and authenticity to the tales. While a character's speech may often reflect regional origins, it also can convey attitudes common in the day. So that readers can better grasp such cultural and historical terms, uncommon words or expressions of the era, the following glossary has been provided.*

abeam: at right angles to the keel of a ship.

account, signing on the: signing the pirate's code and declaring membership with a group of pirates.

Anegada Passage: channel connecting the Atlantic Ocean with the Caribbean Sea. It is forty miles wide and separates the British Virgin Islands from the Caribbean Islands to the south.

astern: in a position behind a specified vessel.

avast: listen; pay attention.

bagnios: slave prisons of Barbary, a region in North Africa extending from west of Egypt to the Atlantic Ocean.

Barbary: Barbary Coast; the term used by Europeans, from the sixteenth until the nineteenth century, to refer to the coastal regions in North Africa that are now Morocco, Algeria, Tunisia and Libya. The name is derived from the Berber people of North Africa. In the West, the name commonly refers to the pirates and slave traders based there.

bark: a sailing ship with three to five masts.

belay: stop.

belaying pin: a large wooden or metal pin that fits into a hole in a rail on a ship or boat, and to which a rope can be fastened.

blackbirder: a person or ship engaged in the slave trade, especially in the Pacific.

Black Ensign: pirates' flag; the flag traditionally flown by a pirate ship, depicting a white skull and crossbones against a black background. Also known as the Jolly Roger.

blackguard: a man who behaves in a dishonorable or contemptible way.

bondmen: in debt bondage, those who are held in servitude by another, without wages or pay, in order to pay off a debt.

bone in her teeth: said of a ship speeding along throwing up spray or foam under the bow.

boucan: smoked beef.

bow chasers: a pair of long guns mounted forward in the bow of a sailing warship to fire directly ahead; used when chasing an enemy to shoot away her sails and rigging.

bowsprit: a spar projecting from the upper end of the bow of a sailing vessel, for holding and supporting a sail.

broadside: all the guns that can be fired from one side of a warship or their simultaneous fire in naval warfare.

buccaneer: from the French word *boucanier*. Boucaniers originally were French hunters in the Caribbean who were poaching cattle and pigs and would smoke the meat on wooden frames called *boucans* so that it could be saved for a later time. Conflict with Spanish forces drove them off the islands and forced them into piracy against the Spanish. The term *buccaneer* was adapted by English settlers, meaning rebel pirates sailing in the Caribbean ports and seas.

bucko: young fellow; chap; young companion.

bulwark: a solid wall enclosing the perimeter of a weather or main deck for the protection of persons or objects on deck.

bumboats: boats used in peddling provisions and small wares among vessels lying in port or offshore.

bunting: flags, especially a vessel's flags collectively.

cable length: a maritime unit of length measuring 720 feet (220 meters) in the US and 608 feet (185 meters) in England.

Castile and León: the territory of the ancient kingdom of León and the northern half of the old kingdom of Castile. Known formally as the Autonomous Community of Castile and León, it is one of the seventeen autonomous communities of Spain, and the largest. Castile and León is divided into nine provinces.

castle: forecastle; the upper deck of a sailing ship, forward of the foremast.

Catherine of Braganza: (1638–1705) born in Portugal, Catherine was the daughter of John IV, the Duke of Braganza (later the King of Portugal). Braganza was the name of a royal dynasty that ruled Portugal from 1640–1910. Catherine was seen as useful in contracting an alliance between Portugal and England, and so the marriage between her and Charles II was arranged. She came to England in 1662.

cat-o'-nine: cat-o'-nine-tails; a whip, usually having nine knotted lines or cords fastened to a handle, used for flogging.

Charlotte Amalie: a Danish colony established in 1672 and named for the Danish queen. It is the largest city in what is now the Virgin Islands.

crosstrees: a pair of horizontal rods attached to a sailing ship's mast to spread the rigging, especially at the head of a topmast.

cutlasses: short, heavy, slightly curved swords with a single cutting edge, formerly used by sailors.

Davy Jones' locker: the ocean's bottom, especially when regarded as the grave of all who perish at sea.

ensign: a naval flag used to indicate nationality.

Execution Dock: located on the Thames River in London, it was a gallows used by the Admiralty (the authority in the UK responsible for the command of the Royal Navy) for over 400 years to hang pirates that had been convicted by its courts and sentenced to die.

filibusteros: (Spanish) filibusters; this term derived from the Spanish *filibustero* for "pirate," "buccaneer" or "freebooter," individuals who attack foreign lands or interests for financial gain without authority from their own government. It first applied to persons raiding Spanish colonies and ships in the West Indies.

flintlock musket: a type of gun fired by a spark from a flint (rock used with steel to produce an igniting spark). A musket is a light gun with a long barrel, fired from the shoulder.

florins: gold or silver coins, especially Dutch coins.

forecastle: the upper deck of a sailing ship, forward of the foremast.

foretop: a platform around the top of a ship's foremast, the mast nearest the front or bow of a vessel with two or more masts.

gaff: a pole rising aft from a mast to support the top of a sail.

galleys: low, flat ships with one or more sails and up to three banks of oars, chiefly used for warfare or piracy and often manned by slaves or criminals.

gentleman-in-waiting: someone who attends a lord or king in some personal matters, or provides personal assistance to lesser members of the family. The gentleman-in-waiting is a subordinate position, however potentially an influential one.

give way: begin to row.

G-men: government men; agents of the Federal Bureau of Investigation.

grape or **grapeshot:** a cluster of small cast-iron balls formerly used as a charge for a cannon.

gun captain: a petty officer in command of a gun crew on a ship.

ha'penny: halfpenny; the British halfpenny coin, no longer used. It took 480 halfpennies to make up a pound sterling.

HMS: His Majesty's Ship.

Isthmus: Isthmus of Panama; a narrow strip of land that lies between the Caribbean Sea and the Pacific Ocean, linking North and South America.

Jacob's ladder: a hanging ladder having ropes or chains supporting wooden or metal rungs or steps.

jibe: to change the course of a ship so that the sails shift from one side of a vessel to the other; said of the sail when the vessel is steered off the wind until the sail fills on the opposite side.

jolly boat: a light boat carried at the stern of a sailing vessel.

keel: a lengthwise structure along the base of a ship, and in some vessels extended downwards as a ridge to increase stability.

King's Letter Boys: midshipmen; a sea officer corps formed by King Charles II of England, as a process of entry and training of new officers. Under this system, young gentlemen of about eleven or twelve years of age were sent to sea with a letter of introduction from the king to learn the ways of the Navy and to grow up in it as a preparation for command. They were known as the "King's Letter Boys" and it gave encouragement to those willing to apply themselves to the learning of navigation and fitting themselves for the service of the sea. This was the channel by which most of the first generation of gentlemen officers first went to sea.

lady-in-waiting: a lady who is in attendance upon a queen or princess.

lanthorn: lantern.

larboard: port side; the left-hand side of a vessel, facing forward.

lighters: large, open, flat-bottomed barges, used in loading and unloading ships offshore or in transporting goods for short distances in shallow waters.

longboat: the longest boat carried by a sailing ship.

luffed: having brought the head of a sailing ship closer to or directly into the wind, with sails shaking.

maintop: a platform at the head of the lower mainmast.

man-o'-war: any armed ship of a national navy, usually carrying between 20 and 120 guns.

marlinespike: a tool made from wood or metal, and used in rope work for tasks such as untwisting rope for splicing or untying knots that tighten up under tension. It is basically a polished cone tapered to a rounded point, usually six to twelve inches long, although sometimes it is longer.

Martinico: Martinique; island in the Caribbean.

matchlock dag: a large pistol with a gunlock (a mechanism to facilitate firing), making it possible to have both hands free to keep a firm grip on the weapon and both eyes on the target.

midshipman: a student naval officer educated principally at sea.

mizzenmast: the third mast from forward in a vessel having three or more masts.

mizzentop: top on the mizzenmast. The *top* is a semicircular platform that rests upon the crosstrees at the head of a lower mast. It serves to spread the topmast shrouds, so as to form a greater angle to the mast and support it better.

Moors: members of a northwest African Muslim people of mixed descent.

morning colors: 8:00 AM when the ensign is hoisted aboard a ship.

Nevis: one of a group of islands extending from Puerto Rico to Martinique in the Caribbean.

¡No me mate! ¡El buque es el suyo!: (Spanish) Don't kill me! The ship is yours!

Nubians: natives or inhabitants of an area of southern Egypt and northern Sudan corresponding to the ancient region of Nubia.

'Od's wounds: by God's wounds; used as an exclamation.

painter: a rope, usually at the bow, for fastening a boat to a ship, stake, etc.

pannikin: a small pan or metal cup.

"pieces of seven": cannons or other types of mounted guns with a bore diameter of seven centimeters.

pipe down for mess: on sailing ships, a pipe (whistle-like device) was used to communicate orders via different arrangements of notes. "Pipe down for mess" was the signal used to announce meals.

pirogues: canoes made by hollowing out tree trunks; dugouts.

points: a point is 11.25 degrees on a compass. Sailing within two points of a breeze refers to sailing within 22.50 degrees of the direction of the wind.

powder monkeys: boys employed on warships to carry gunpowder from the magazine to the guns.

press gang: a body of persons under the command of an officer, formerly employed to impress others for service, especially in the navy or army.

press ganging: forcing (a person) into military or naval service.

put in: to enter a port or harbor, especially for shelter, repairs or provisions.

quarters, sound: call or summon the ship's crew to their assigned stations or posts.

¿Quién es?: (Spanish) Who is that?

rag: a sail or any piece of canvas.

rapier: a small sword, especially of the eighteenth century, having a narrow blade and used for thrusting.

reef: to reduce the area of a sail by gathering part of it in.

Saint George, cross of: red cross on a white field used on the flag of Great Britain.

Scheherazade: the female narrator of *The Arabian Nights*, who during one thousand and one adventurous nights saved her life by entertaining her husband, the king, with stories.

scuppers: openings in the side of a ship at deck level that allow water to run off.

scurvy: a disease caused by a deficiency of vitamin C, characterized by bleeding gums and the opening of previously healed wounds.

sea artist: a ship's navigator.

Sennar: a Muslim kingdom that extended over most of the eastern part of the present Sudan, a country in northeast Africa.

serpentines: cannons of various bore sizes, used from the fifteenth to the seventeenth century.

ship-rigged: describes a sailing ship with three, four or five masts and square sails set at right angles to the hull.

shrouds: supporting ropes or wires that extend down from the top of a mast.

signal ratchet: a device used to restrict motion in one direction. Ratchets work by having a form of gearwheel with the teeth set off at an angle, and a protrusion that rests against the gearwheel. When the gearwheel is rotated in one direction, the protrusion raises and clicks back in place, keeping it from making a backward motion. Continuous motion in the one direction makes a clicking sound. A signal ratchet is used to raise a signal flag.

sirrah: a term of address used to inferiors or children to express impatience, contempt, etc.

slaver: a slave ship; a ship for transporting slaves from their native homes to places of bondage.

spar: a thick, strong pole, especially one used as a mast to hold the sails on a ship.

sprit: a small pole running diagonally from the foot of a mast up to the top corner of a fore-and-aft sail, to support and stretch it.

spritsails: sails that are extended by being mounted on a sprit.

stand on and off: to keep at a safe distance; to sail alternately toward and away from shore so as to keep a point in sight.

stay: any of various strong ropes or wires for steadying masts.

stepped: placed in its step (the block in which the heel of the mast is fixed).

sterncastle: raised deck at the stern serving as the ship's command center during most actions. The pilot guides the ship from a large wheel there, while the captain looks over and directs the crew working above deck.

stern chaser: a cannon mounted at or near the stern of a sailing ship, facing aft.

struck colors: "striking the colors"; the universally recognized indication of surrender. The colors, a national flag or a battle ensign, are hauled down as a token of submission.

sweeps: long, heavy oars.

tacking: changing course by turning a boat's head into and through the wind; making a series of such changes of course while sailing.

taffrail: a rail above the stern of a ship.

thwarts: seats across a boat, especially those used by rowers.

Toledo: Toledo, Spain; a city renowned for making swords of finely tempered steel.

touchholes: the vents in the breeches of early firearms or cannons through which the charge was ignited.

trade wind: a nearly constant easterly wind that dominates most of the tropics and subtropics throughout the world, blowing mainly from the northeast in the Northern Hemisphere, and from the southeast in the Southern Hemisphere.

truck: a piece of wood fixed at the top of a mast, usually having holes through which ropes can be passed to raise or lower the sails.

Tunisia: a country situated on the Mediterranean coast of North Africa.

'tween decks: between decks; spaces between two continuous decks in the hull of a vessel.

under weigh: in motion; underway.

Valhalla: (Norse mythology) the great hall where the souls of heroes killed in battle spend eternity.

waist: the central part of a ship.

weigh anchor: take up the anchor when ready to sail.

whelp: a youth, especially an impudent or despised one.

yardarm: either end of a long, slender beam or pole that supports a square sail.

FULL-RIGGED SAILING SHIP

1: flying jib
2: jib
3: fore-topmast staysail
4: foresail
5: lower fore-topsail
6: upper fore-topsail
7: fore-topgallant sail
8: fore-royal
9: fore-skysail
10: lower studding sail
    (never on the main)
11: fore-topmast studding sail
12: fore-topgallant studding sail
13: fore-royal studding sail
14: main staysail
15: main-topmast staysail
16: main-topgallant staysail
17: main-royal staysail
18: mainsail

19: lower main topsail
20: upper main topsail
21: main-topgallant sail
22: main royal
23: main skysail
24: main-topmast studding sail
25: main-topgallant studding sail
26: main-royal studding sail
27: mizzen staysail
28: mizzen-topmast staysail
29: mizzen-topgallant staysail
30: mizzen-royal staysail
31: mizzen sail (crossjack)
32: lower mizzen topsail
33: upper mizzen topsail
34: mizzen-topgallant sail
35: mizzen royal
36: mizzen skysail
37: spanker

L. Ron Hubbard
in the Golden Age
of Pulp Fiction

*In writing an adventure story
a writer has to know that he is adventuring
for a lot of people who cannot.
The writer has to take them here and there
about the globe and show them
excitement and love and realism.
As long as that writer is living the part of an
adventurer when he is hammering
the keys, he is succeeding with his story.*

*Adventuring is a state of mind.
If you adventure through life, you have a
good chance to be a success on paper.*

*Adventure doesn't mean globe-trotting,
exactly, and it doesn't mean great deeds.
Adventuring is like art.
You have to live it to make it real.*

—L. RON HUBBARD

L. Ron Hubbard
and American
Pulp Fiction

B ORN March 13, 1911, L. Ron Hubbard lived a life at least as expansive as the stories with which he enthralled a hundred million readers through a fifty-year career.

Originally hailing from Tilden, Nebraska, he spent his formative years in a classically rugged Montana, replete with the cowpunchers, lawmen and desperadoes who would later people his Wild West adventures. And lest anyone imagine those adventures were drawn from vicarious experience, he was not only breaking broncs at a tender age, he was also among the few whites ever admitted into Blackfoot society as a bona fide blood brother. While if only to round out an otherwise rough and tumble youth, his mother was that rarity of her time—a thoroughly educated woman—who introduced her son to the classics of Occidental literature even before his seventh birthday.

But as any dedicated L. Ron Hubbard reader will attest, his world extended far beyond Montana. In point of fact, and as the son of a United States naval officer, by the age of eighteen he had traveled over a quarter of a million miles. Included therein were three Pacific crossings to a then still mysterious Asia, where he ran with the likes of Her British Majesty's agent-in-place

L. Ron Hubbard, left, at Congressional Airport, Washington, DC, 1931, with members of George Washington University flying club.

for North China, and the last in the line of Royal Magicians from the court of Kublai Khan. For the record, L. Ron Hubbard was also among the first Westerners to gain admittance to forbidden Tibetan monasteries below Manchuria, and his photographs of China's Great Wall long graced American geography texts.

Upon his return to the United States and a hasty completion of his interrupted high school education, the young Ron Hubbard entered George Washington University. There, as fans of his aerial adventures may have heard, he earned his wings as a pioneering barnstormer at the dawn of American aviation. He also earned a place in free-flight record books for the longest sustained flight above Chicago. Moreover, as a roving reporter for *Sportsman Pilot* (featuring his first professionally penned articles), he further helped inspire a generation of pilots who would take America to world airpower.

Immediately beyond his sophomore year, Ron embarked on the first of his famed ethnological expeditions, initially to then untrammeled Caribbean shores (descriptions of which would later fill a whole series of West Indies mystery-thrillers). That the Puerto Rican interior would also figure into the future of Ron Hubbard stories was likewise no accident. For in addition to cultural studies of the island, a 1932–33

LRH expedition is rightly remembered as conducting the first complete mineralogical survey of a Puerto Rico under United States jurisdiction.

There was many another adventure along this vein: As a lifetime member of the famed Explorers Club, L. Ron Hubbard charted North Pacific waters with the first shipboard radio direction finder, and so pioneered a long-range navigation system universally employed until the late twentieth century. While not to put too fine an edge on it, he also held a rare Master Mariner's license to pilot any vessel, of any tonnage in any ocean.

Yet lest we stray too far afield, there is an LRH note at this juncture in his saga, and it reads in part:

"I started out writing for the pulps, writing the best I knew, writing for every mag on the stands, slanting as well as I could."

To which one might add: His earliest submissions date from the

Capt. L. Ron Hubbard in Ketchikan, Alaska, 1940, on his Alaskan Radio Experimental Expedition, the first of three voyages conducted under the Explorers Club flag.

summer of 1934, and included tales drawn from true-to-life Asian adventures, with characters roughly modeled on British/American intelligence operatives he had known in Shanghai. His early Westerns were similarly peppered with details drawn from personal experience. Although therein lay a first hard lesson from the often cruel world of the pulps. His first Westerns were soundly rejected as lacking the authenticity of a Max Brand yarn (a particularly frustrating comment given L. Ron Hubbard's Westerns came straight from his Montana homeland, while Max Brand was a mediocre New York poet named Frederick Schiller Faust, who turned out implausible six-shooter tales from the terrace of an Italian villa).

Nevertheless, and needless to say, L. Ron Hubbard persevered and soon earned a reputation as among the most publishable names in pulp fiction, with a ninety percent placement rate of first-draft manuscripts. He was also among the most prolific, averaging between seventy and a hundred thousand words a month. Hence the rumors that L. Ron Hubbard had redesigned a typewriter for faster keyboard action and pounded out manuscripts on a continuous roll of butcher paper to save the precious seconds it took to insert a single sheet of paper into manual typewriters of the day.

That all L. Ron Hubbard stories did not run beneath said byline is yet another aspect of pulp fiction lore. That is, as publishers periodically rejected manuscripts from top-drawer authors if only to avoid paying top dollar, L. Ron Hubbard and company just as frequently replied with submissions under various pseudonyms. In Ron's case, the

A MAN OF MANY NAMES

Between 1934 and 1950, L. Ron Hubbard authored more than fifteen million words of fiction in more than two hundred classic publications. To supply his fans and editors with stories across an array of genres and pulp titles, he adopted fifteen pseudonyms in addition to his already renowned L. Ron Hubbard byline.

Winchester Remington Colt
Lt. Jonathan Daly
Capt. Charles Gordon
Capt. L. Ron Hubbard
Bernard Hubbel
Michael Keith
Rene Lafayette
Legionnaire 148
Legionnaire 14830
Ken Martin
Scott Morgan
Lt. Scott Morgan
Kurt von Rachen
Barry Randolph
Capt. Humbert Reynolds

list included: Rene Lafayette, Captain Charles Gordon, Lt. Scott Morgan and the notorious Kurt von Rachen—supposedly on the lam for a murder rap, while hammering out two-fisted prose in Argentina. The point: While L. Ron Hubbard as Ken Martin spun stories of Southeast Asian intrigue, LRH as Barry Randolph authored tales of romance on the Western range—which, stretching between a dozen genres is how he came to stand among the two hundred elite authors providing close to a million tales through the glory days of American Pulp Fiction.

L. Ron Hubbard, circa 1930, at the outset of a literary career that would finally span half a century.

In evidence of exactly that, by 1936 L. Ron Hubbard was literally leading pulp fiction's elite as president of New York's American Fiction Guild. Members included a veritable pulp hall of fame: Lester "Doc Savage" Dent, Walter "The Shadow" Gibson, and the legendary Dashiell Hammett—to cite but a few.

Also in evidence of just where L. Ron Hubbard stood within his first two years on the American pulp circuit: By the spring of 1937, he was ensconced in Hollywood, adopting a Caribbean thriller for Columbia Pictures, remembered today as *The Secret of Treasure Island*. Comprising fifteen thirty-minute episodes, the L. Ron Hubbard screenplay led to the most profitable matinée serial in Hollywood history. In accord with Hollywood culture, he was thereafter continually called upon

The 1937 Secret of Treasure Island, *a fifteen-episode serial adapted for the screen by L. Ron Hubbard from his novel,* Murder at Pirate Castle.

to rewrite/doctor scripts—most famously for long-time friend and fellow adventurer Clark Gable.

In the interim—and herein lies another distinctive chapter of the L. Ron Hubbard story—he continually worked to open Pulp Kingdom gates to up-and-coming authors. Or, for that matter, anyone who wished to write. It was a fairly unconventional stance, as markets were already thin and competition razor sharp. But the fact remains, it was an L. Ron Hubbard hallmark that he vehemently lobbied on behalf of young authors—regularly supplying instructional articles to trade journals, guest-lecturing to short story classes at George Washington University and Harvard, and even founding his own creative writing competition. It was established in 1940, dubbed the Golden Pen, and guaranteed winners both New York representation and publication in *Argosy*.

But it was John W. Campbell Jr.'s *Astounding Science Fiction* that finally proved the most memorable LRH vehicle. While every fan of L. Ron Hubbard's galactic epics undoubtedly knows the story, it nonetheless bears repeating: By late 1938, the pulp publishing magnate of Street & Smith was determined to revamp *Astounding Science Fiction* for broader readership. In particular, senior editorial director F. Orlin Tremaine called for stories with a stronger *human element*. When acting editor John W. Campbell balked, preferring his spaceship-driven tales, Tremaine enlisted Hubbard. Hubbard, in turn, replied with the genre's first truly *character-driven* works, wherein heroes are pitted not against bug-eyed monsters but the mystery and majesty of deep space itself—and thus was launched the Golden Age of Science Fiction.

The names alone are enough to quicken the pulse of any science fiction aficionado, including LRH friend and protégé, Robert Heinlein, Isaac Asimov, A. E. van Vogt and Ray Bradbury. Moreover, when coupled with LRH stories of fantasy, we further come to what's rightly been described as the foundation of every modern tale of horror: L. Ron Hubbard's immortal *Fear*. It was rightly proclaimed by Stephen King as one of the very few works to genuinely warrant that overworked term "classic"—as in: *"This is a classic tale of creeping, surreal menace and horror. . . . This is one of the really, really good ones."*

L. Ron Hubbard, 1948, among fellow science fiction luminaries at the World Science Fiction Convention in Toronto.

To accommodate the greater body of L. Ron Hubbard fantasies, Street & Smith inaugurated *Unknown*—a classic pulp if there ever was one, and wherein readers were soon thrilling to the likes of *Typewriter in the Sky* and *Slaves of Sleep* of which Frederik Pohl would declare: *"There are bits and pieces from Ron's work that became part of the language in ways that very few other writers managed."*

And, indeed, at J. W. Campbell Jr.'s insistence, Ron was regularly drawing on themes from the Arabian Nights and so introducing readers to a world of genies, jinn, Aladdin and Sinbad—all of which, of course, continue to float through cultural mythology to this day.

At least as influential in terms of post-apocalypse stories was L. Ron Hubbard's 1940 *Final Blackout*. Generally acclaimed as the finest anti-war novel of the decade and among the ten best works of the genre ever authored—here, too, was a tale that would live on in ways few other writers imagined.

Hence, the later Robert Heinlein verdict: "Final Blackout *is as perfect a piece of science fiction as has ever been written.*"

Like many another who both lived and wrote American pulp adventure, the war proved a tragic end to Ron's sojourn in the pulps. He served with distinction in four theaters and was highly decorated for commanding corvettes in the North Pacific. He was also grievously wounded in combat, lost many a close friend and colleague and thus resolved to say farewell to pulp fiction and devote himself to what it had supported these many years—namely, his serious research.

Portland, Oregon, 1943; L. Ron Hubbard, captain of the US Navy subchaser PC 815.

But in no way was the LRH literary saga at an end, for as he wrote some thirty years later, in 1980:

"Recently there came a period when I had little to do. This was novel in a life so crammed with busy years, and I decided to amuse myself by writing a novel that was pure science fiction."

That work was *Battlefield Earth: A Saga of the Year 3000*. It was an immediate *New York Times* bestseller and, in fact, the first international science fiction blockbuster in decades. It was not, however, L. Ron Hubbard's magnum opus, as that distinction is generally reserved for his next and final work: The 1.2 million word *Mission Earth*.

> **Final Blackout**
> *is as perfect a piece of science fiction as has ever been written.*
>
> —Robert Heinlein

How he managed those 1.2 million words in just over twelve months is yet another piece of the L. Ron Hubbard legend. But the fact remains, he did indeed author a ten-volume *dekalogy* that lives in publishing history for the fact that each and every volume of the series was also a *New York Times* bestseller.

Moreover, as subsequent generations discovered L. Ron Hubbard through republished works and novelizations of his screenplays, the mere fact of his name on a cover signaled an international bestseller. . . . Until, to date, sales of his works exceed hundreds of millions, and he otherwise remains among the most enduring and widely read authors in literary history. Although as a final word on the tales of L. Ron Hubbard, perhaps it's enough to simply reiterate what editors told readers in the glory days of American Pulp Fiction:

He writes the way he does, brothers, because he's been there, seen it and done it!

THE STORIES FROM THE GOLDEN AGE

Your ticket to adventure starts here with the Stories from
the Golden Age collection by master storyteller L. Ron Hubbard.
These gripping tales are set in a kaleidoscope of exotic locales and brim
with fascinating characters, including some of the
most vile villains, dangerous dames and brazen heroes
you'll ever get to meet.

The entire collection of over one hundred and fifty stories is being
released in a series of eighty books and audiobooks.
For an up-to-date listing of available titles,
go to www.goldenagestories.com.

AIR ADVENTURE

Arctic Wings   *Man-Killers of the Air*
The Battling Pilot   *On Blazing Wings*
Boomerang Bomber   *Red Death Over China*
The Crate Killer   *Sabotage in the Sky*
The Dive Bomber   *Sky Birds Dare!*
Forbidden Gold   *The Sky-Crasher*
Hurtling Wings   *Trouble on His Wings*
The Lieutenant Takes the Sky *Wings Over Ethiopia*

117

FAR-FLUNG ADVENTURE

The Adventure of "X"
All Frontiers Are Jealous
The Barbarians
The Black Sultan
Black Towers to Danger
The Bold Dare All
Buckley Plays a Hunch
The Cossack
Destiny's Drum
Escape for Three
Fifty-Fifty O'Brien
The Headhunters
Hell's Legionnaire
He Walked to War
Hostage to Death

Hurricane
The Iron Duke
Machine Gun 21,000
Medals for Mahoney
Price of a Hat
Red Sand
The Sky Devil
The Small Boss of Nunaloha
The Squad That Never Came Back
Starch and Stripes
Tomb of the Ten Thousand Dead
Trick Soldier
While Bugles Blow!
Yukon Madness

SEA ADVENTURE

Cargo of Coffins
The Drowned City
False Cargo
Grounded
Loot of the Shanung
Mister Tidwell, Gunner

The Phantom Patrol
Sea Fangs
Submarine
Twenty Fathoms Down
Under the Black Ensign

TALES FROM THE ORIENT

The Devil—With Wings

The Falcon Killer

Five Mex for a Million

Golden Hell

The Green God

Hurricane's Roar

Inky Odds

Orders Is Orders

Pearl Pirate

The Red Dragon

Spy Killer

Tah

The Trail of the Red Diamonds

Wind-Gone-Mad

Yellow Loot

MYSTERY

The Blow Torch Murder

Brass Keys to Murder

Calling Squad Cars!

The Carnival of Death

The Chee-Chalker

Dead Men Kill

The Death Flyer

Flame City

The Grease Spot

Killer Ape

Killer's Law

The Mad Dog Murder

Mouthpiece

Murder Afloat

The Slickers

They Killed Him Dead

FANTASY

Borrowed Glory   If I Were You
The Crossroads   The Last Drop
Danger in the Dark   The Room
The Devil's Rescue   The Tramp
He Didn't Like Cats

SCIENCE FICTION

The Automagic Horse   A Matter of Matter
Battle of Wizards   The Obsolete Weapon
Battling Bolto   One Was Stubborn
The Beast   The Planet Makers
Beyond All Weapons   The Professor Was a Thief
A Can of Vacuum   The Slaver
The Conroy Diary   Space Can
The Dangerous Dimension   Strain
Final Enemy   Tough Old Man
The Great Secret   240,000 Miles Straight Up
Greed   When Shadows Fall
The Invaders

WESTERN

The Baron of Coyote River	*Man for Breakfast*
Blood on His Spurs	*The No-Gun Gunhawk*
Boss of the Lazy B	*The No-Gun Man*
Branded Outlaw	*The Ranch That No One Would Buy*
Cattle King for a Day	*Reign of the Gila Monster*
Come and Get It	*Ride 'Em, Cowboy*
Death Waits at Sundown	*Ruin at Rio Piedras*
Devil's Manhunt	*Shadows from Boot Hill*
The Ghost Town Gun-Ghost	*Silent Pards*
Gun Boss of Tumbleweed	*Six-Gun Caballero*
Gunman!	*Stacked Bullets*
Gunman's Tally	*Stranger in Town*
The Gunner from Gehenna	*Tinhorn's Daughter*
Hoss Tamer	*The Toughest Ranger*
Johnny, the Town Tamer	*Under the Diehard Brand*
King of the Gunmen	*Vengeance Is Mine!*
The Magic Quirt	*When Gilhooly Was in Flower*

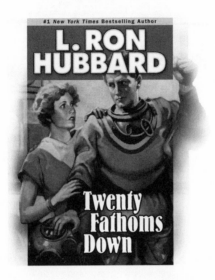